MOUNTAIN BLOOD

Will Baker

A TOUCHSTONE BOOK
Published by Simon & Schuster Inc.
New York • London • Toronto • Sydney • Tokyo

Touchstone
Simon & Schuster Building
Rockefeller Center
1230 Avenue of the Americas
New York, New York 10020

First Touchstone Edition, 1988

Published by arrangement with University of Georgia Press

TOUCHSTONE and colophon are registered trademarks of Simon &
Schuster Inc.

Designed by Sandra Strother Hudson

Manufactured in the United States of America

1   3   5   7   9   10   8   6   4   2

Library of Congress Cataloging in Publication Data

ISBN 0-671-66096-9 Pbk.

Grateful acknowledgement is made to the editors of the publications in
which the following stories first appeared: "The Winged Worm," *Pacific
Northwest Review*; "The Beautician and the One-Legged Man," *Missouri Review*; "The Legend of Great Uncle Jim and the Woman Behind
It All," *Co-Evolution Quarterly*; "Letter to a Nebraska Housewife,"
Akwasasne Notes; "Sourdoughs, Filibusters, and a One-Eared Mule,"
The Georgia Review; "Father White Mouse," *Outside*.

ACKNOWLEDGMENTS

I am indebted to a number of people, places, and books for help in the preparation of these pages. Deanie Roush, Jim Webb, Malinda Penn, Muriel Wakazoo, and the people of Otíka supplied hospitality, food, and companionship. Meadows Valley, Long Valley, and the Deadwood Basin nurtured a special breed of hardy individualists whose memory inspired many of the tales included here. A few facts cited in the "Letter to a Nebraska Housewife" come from James Mooney's *The Ghost Dance Religion* and Truman Capote's *In Cold Blood.* For much of the exotic material in the final essay I relied on three books: Jenifer Marx's *The Magic of Gold,* Timothy Green's *The New World of Gold,* and Alex Del Mar's *A History of the Precious Metals.*

CONTENTS

This song is for the crazy, greedy, doomed lovers of wild things.

INTRODUCTION

Readers have a right to know what kind of book they are up against, in a general way. That can be taken care of with a cover design (guns, flames, half-dressed women) and a phrase ("Saga of Doom and Desire," "Epic of Passion"), or a title so formidable that no one could mistake its drift (*The Origin of Consciousness in the Breakdown of the Bicameral Mind*). Such works librarians catalogue swiftly. If there is any doubt—a missing dust jacket or a trendy, ambiguous title—they can glance at the bio sketch or the list of previous publications to see what the author has been doing recently.

One distinction, however, seems to be especially important: that between fact and fiction. If a thing happened and is true, then it belongs with history, autobiography, science. If it didn't, or didn't quite that way, then we are dealing with fiction, the imagination, or (in one of the more barbarous phrases of modern pedagogy) "creative writing." Many people are fanatical about maintaining this line of demarcation. What *really* happened is not to be corrupted by some effete wordsmith, who exaggerates or suppresses to suit his own devious ends. On the other hand, as long as a book offers itself openly as "just a story," these people will not only accept but favor all kinds of absurdities. The man who fumes if a sportswriter misspells a second-stringer's name may relish an account of intelligent blue fungus from another galaxy.

There are good reasons why people dislike any confusion of the real and the imaginary. Sometimes a public record or reputation is at stake. False and malicious innuendo might ruin a career or policy, so the lawsuit for slander or libel depends upon getting at just what was said, done, or thought. And in

1

the case of scientific or engineering knowledge, purveying inaccuracies can bring about worse disasters: the bridge collapses or the patient dies. In addition, most of us have an aversion to the cunning liar whose purpose is to bamboozle us to advance his own interest, and we respect those who will admit and correct an error even at their own expense.

Americans like to think of themselves as a pragmatic, straightforward people. They deal in clear categories (like Good vs. Communism). They don't readily tolerate superstitious flummery or contorted intellectualization, because they rightly perceive that these are often a pose to conceal selfish designs. Especially when there is money on the line, we want the plain facts. The salt, sugar, vitamin C, and diglycerides must be listed right there on the package.

When it comes to the fantastic side of life, however, Americans are just as big liars as the rest of the world. Possibly bigger. Paul Bunyan and Mike Fink and Davey Crockett are barely venerable enough to be folk heroes; the unkind might call them plain baloney. Our popular art—I am thinking mostly of soap operas, cinema, and supermarket magazines—is full of the most outrageous sentimentality, the most incredible exaggeration. Here the hard-headed Yankee grows uncritical, if not gullible. Gee, he or she says, what a wonderful, scary, thrilling, amazing, fascinating, moving story that was. I wonder if it's based on real life?

Still more marvelous, as the populace absorbs this guff they try to live up—or down—to it. Life begins to imitate the outrageous and incredible. CIA secret agents try to poison Fidel Castro's cigars. Lovesick swain shoots president. Heroic doctor implants baboon heart in new baby. People captured by UFO are grilled for hours. Lesbian couples inseminate each other with turkey basters full of homosexual sperm. There seems to be no invention so farfetched that some enthusiast cannot live out a fair copy of it. The *National Enquirer* may eventually run the *New York Times* out of business, because they will be printing the same material.

Perhaps this intrusion of fancy into daily life is one reason people want, more than ever, certification of what is true and what is made up. The trouble is, in certain areas like advertising and politics (if these are separable any more) fabrication is so ingenious and widespread that, as people commonly put it, you don't know what to believe. Such uncertainty leads eventually to believing nothing or believing (fanatically) whatever suits you, and most of us can sense the danger of those positions. Consequently a writer is now likely to confront a public either suspicious or nonchalant: the reader is thinking either "You better not fudge your data, Mr. Expert," or "Let's see what kind of bull this clown has to offer." Either way, the storyteller is on immediate probation, and is expected to give a clear signal of intentions. Fact or fiction.

Nevertheless, I must confess straight out that I can't comfortably put *Mountain Blood* in one or the other of these important classifications. In certain stories, the ones about Father White Mouse and my Aunt Nellie and Great Uncle Jim, I did try to report the facts and exactly how I felt about them. In others, like the tale of the Beautician and the One-Legged Man and the Letter to a Nebraska Housewife, I imagined a good deal around central events that actually happened, or I made things happen in a different order. The overall slant of the book is definitely toward truth—a certain kind of truth—but I don't claim scrupulous accuracy, and terms like *yarn* or *essay* or *memoir* or *meditation* would help only a little, even though there are elements of all these approaches in what follows.

I don't think I'm alone in this dilemma. We have seen an interesting miscegenation of genres in the last couple of decades. Now we can have imaginary people in real gardens (most Michener books) or real people in imaginary scenes (Doctorow, Coover, Vidal). Capote and Mailer have used the techniques and style of the novel—gothic thriller and urban naturalism—on actual people in this given world. Hunter Thompson, Edward Abbey, and Tom Wolfe (and their disciples) have twisted documentary journalism until it now regularly includes the reporter's inner life, his phobias and fantasies and hallucinations. Even scientists, especially naturalists and anthropologists, have been cultivating the intensely personal, eyewitness account (Eisely, Matthiessen, Turnbull).

3

The approach in this new material is not so radically different from that of past writers (Montaigne, Lamb, Carlyle, Twain), but what was formerly an element of charm, eccentricity, or playfulness, has become a crucial component of form. The subjectivity of new journalism and the urge to load information into novels are both ways of dealing with our awareness of an omnipresent and treacherous interpenetration of inner and outer worlds. We have learned that institutes can grind out statistics—all reliable—to prove any "point of view"; that every fact has been presented to us by a subtle, invisible hand; that beneath the airy fancies of our fabulists lurk specific private obsessions; that dedication speeches, schoolbooks, fairy tales, repair manuals, bomb-shelter symbols, and introductions can also grind axes. The most honest solution seems to be, ironically, for the writer to inject his biases into the work in an unmistakable way, to objectify his subjectivity, to manifest for the reader a free commerce between the real world and the phantasmagoria of mental life.

In my sporadic reading on the matter, I find that this approach is often traced to Immanuel Kant, who, as far as I understand him, argues that it is *all* made up. The hardheaded scientific proof and the poet's crazed song are equally pure constructs of the tricky human brain. We make whatever sense is to be made out of things, and without us none of it makes any sense at all. Man said, "Let there be phenomena," and everything was. Volumes have been written to elaborate or modify this disturbing proposition, but it appears to have held up. Quarks and black holes are inventions as daring as any artist's dream, and the found or concrete poem has all the presence of a hunk of magnetite.

My perspective on this deep and complicated issue is very rudimentary and involves not written but unwritten volumes. I begin with what I believe is a common human experience. Our primal confusion is succeeded by a brief interlude of lucidity, before we plunge into the still greater confusion of adult life. For example, everyone laughed when, as soon as we got control of a few words, we made up tales about the man in the moon or monsters we talked to and tamed in the dead of night. But then everyone frowned if we made up convincing accounts of how those scratches came to be on the car hood or how certain items vanished from our sister's drawer. After we were straightened out, we knew the difference between fantasizing for sheer fun (good) and lying to escape punishment (bad). The trouble was, this distinction did not by any means clear up all the interesting cases.

We soon became aware of how grownups fibbed to each other all the time, in ways that were apparently held to be acceptable or even admirable. No one, for example, told the truth about a woman's hairdo or what a horse was worth. Sometimes events to which we were actual eyewitnesses were unrecognizable when our parents retailed them. Even our own exploits grew in stature, developed frames and frills. Eventually we learned how to perform this subtle alchemy ourselves. We discovered the effect of the pregnant detail, how to highlight and shade artfully, when we could invent. You could get away with a lot, we saw, behind phrases like "She must have . . ." or "I suppose they were . . ."

Some were really good at this kind of elaboration, and for those chosen or cursed few, life would never be the same. In the carny show of twentieth-century America they could do very well (as lawyers or salespersons) but they also risked losing the chief props of a comfortable, bourgeois existence. They risked becoming fatally, perversely addicted to their own gift for its own sake; they might try to become artists, hence in penurious bondage to a lonely, morally ambiguous craft.

For one thing the rankest beginner grasps is that the telling is all. In Conrad's words, "the *whole* of the truth lies in the presentation." Without his tongue of fire, the prophet can muff even revelation, and the faithful will blaspheme with their yawns. Any hard-working, intelligent person can do a fair job of organizing and presenting facts, and if the facts happen to be an angel's visit or the sinking of the Titanic or the life of Rasputin, the resulting account has a chance of being interesting, even thrilling. But the student of these matters sees soon enough that a master can transform even trivial events or notions—the near-collision of two carriages, a contest of leaping amphibians—into immortal works of art.

5

This is true even at the level of mere narrative carpentry. The shaping of sentences, a shrewd management of adjectives, even a comma, dash, or period can lend emotional color or whet interest. Think of what Hemingway does with his *and*'s and *the*'s, or James with his clauses cantilevered out over a syntactic abyss. One learns that people will pay for this skill, which can be injected into anything from government reports and afterdinner speeches to bedtime stories and love letters (though it is difficult to market in its pure form, as poetry). The thoughtful apprentice develops an uneasy suspicion: the mastery of this strange power requires forsaking fidelity to those hard-won childhood concepts of truth, especially truth as some function of "what really happened."

Why? Because this mastery in its supreme form creates its own truth, determines the "what" of what happened. Matched with a grand subject, it may fabricate great art—major novels, authoritative biographies and histories, landmark essays—or, alternately, it may generate the most magnificent humbug. It is not easy—it may in fact be impossible—to tell one from the other. The gifted storyteller is like a fine actor, who can persuade us of the pathos or heroism or general gravity of almost any little business, just by the way he drops a certain word, rounds a particular phrase, shrugs, or clenches his fist.

The phenomenon is clearest in poetry, where "truth" hasn't much to do with what the words ostensibly mean. A poet can call an old man a stick or a bare tree a ruined church or evening a man lying in a coma, and the professors tell us these stretchers are even the highest, purest kind of truth, an ultimate fidelity to feeling. It is all right for the poet to take all manner of outrageous figures and cast them in a musical pattern quite unlike what anybody really sounds like, and the verdict is that these compositions convey a direct, authentic, and powerful sort of veracity: Beauty is Truth, Truth Beauty. The moral imagination, and so forth.

The workman in prose doesn't usually have that kind of license, but in one of its humbler forms there is a strong parallel to this exalted aesthetic. Much of what I have said so far about the shifty ground between fact and fiction applies mostly to the written word (especially the unease and skepticism of the modern reader, the insistent exhibitionism of the modern writer), but suppose we turn to a much larger—probably universal—and equally active tradition to which, despite its somewhat pompous title, most of us contribute.

This is the oral tradition. We hear and pass on by word of mouth all kinds of stories: gossip, jokes, shop talk, travelogues, our condensed life history to seatmates on a long flight. Out of this gab we occasionally select an anecdote because it has some extraordinary impact, and through numerous tellings it begins to acquire a shape, a design, a depth only dimly perceived at first. There are no records, no transcripts or tapes or video footage to constrict us, so details tend to appear, alter, and vanish according to the subterranean whims of artistic judgment. Before long we are on the fringe of what we call legend, the tale that seems too good or too terrible to be entirely true, but which has nonetheless a mysterious, authentic vitality.

This process is a commonplace and admirable demonstration of the principle that we make up the world to suit ourselves. What experience gives us we rework instinctively, the imagination definitely in play, and our auditors may take the same license and transform the material yet again. The telling and retelling can go on for generations; and on this uncertain terrain, verifiable fact almost ceases to exist: all is memory, hearsay, clever interpolation.

All the same there are rough limits, a sort of genre, a few classics. Examples can of course be found in the oral history sections of county libraries, but accomplished writers are also working this vein: Ivan Doig, *This House of Sky;* Barry Holstun Lopez, *Winter Count;* Norman Maclean, *A River Runs Through It* (all three writing of a place that bears the Spanish name for mountain). Often these stories on their way to becoming legends are part of a family archive, are told by the old to the young as a homage to ancestors and a way of connecting generations. Hence the most dramatic and important persons and events are rooted in actuality. Births and deaths are perhaps recorded on the flyleaf of an old Bible, and memories of emigration can be inexorably tied to great political or social events—the gold rush or the

Homestead Act or the dustbowl. Also, by convention, the elders of a tribe have a special authority, and a special responsibility to curb the wildest guesswork of their kin, or to adjudicate between conflicting versions of a tale.

But around and between these few guidelines the imagination is free to trade. In fact, it must do so, if the stories are to come alive and fascinate the young. Some careful aunts will embroider only a very little and spend their energies in watchful demolition of dangerous male bombast, and an occasional grandparent will devote every effort to clipping newspapers and saving snapshots, thus cataloguing and fixing some final, indisputable chronicle, but always the process will go on: the trimming and grafting and fumbling and weighing and throwing out of material in search of the right combination—perhaps just that so-called higher truth of the poets, though in a different medium with different rules.

My guess is that everybody inherits a stock of such stories and everybody at some point adds to that stock. Everybody is sometimes subject, sometimes weaver, and sometimes in between. Most of us, for example, are tantalized by certain anecdotes about ourselves: we can't tell whether we actually recall them or have heard them so often they seem to be our own experience. Anyway, in telling them, we *make* them our experience.

In large families, after many years, it can happen that nobody is absolutely sure of who did what to whom when—whether it was Geraldine or Mary Lou who scalded the baby, and whether that happened before or after the big flood—while in other cases everybody agrees—nobody will ever forget—how Brother Bob saw the boar and seized the pitchfork and . . . so forth. If a family is so large as to approach tribal status, and garrulous besides, this editorial inconsistency is greatly enhanced. Inevitably some well-meaning raconteur begins to fool with the chronology and cast of an affair, trying perhaps to introduce a little order to resolve contradictions, and—by a process we have already outlined—ends by sacrificing his integrity on the altar of art. If he tells a good enough story, nobody much cares.

This oral tradition in a rural context is the background for most of the stories collected here, and influences all of them. I grew up in a small back-woods community, before television, so a winter evening's entertainment usually consisted of listening to my relatives regale each other with tales, old and new. The scene is sketched at the opening of "Sourdoughs, Fil-ibusters, and a One-Eared Mule," but it could serve to introduce the other stories as well. I learned in these sessions something about complex nar-rative, about the relativity of truth, and about how a small boy can be led from curiosity through wonder to utter thralldom. I suppose I was also ab-sorbing—though God knows I could never have guessed—the elements of Kant's philosophy. At any rate I acquired a view of facts as only the neces-sary seed for flowers of the imagination, and therefore have no compunction about nourishing these blooms with the wind and fertilizer of literary style.

I expect to hear from a couple of irate aunts, and perhaps from some peripheral characters whose names I may have switched around, and just possibly from the law firm representing the Homestake Mining Corporation; but I cite my Grandmother Minnie, now ten years gone, as precedent for whatever liberties of expression I have taken. Once a very distant Texas cousin of Grandfather's dropped in for a visit. Unpacking his bedroll and rifle from a Model A, this old renegade drank a half case of beer and kept us up half the night with tales of the Spanish American War and his ten years in prison ("accidental" homicide, he called it). Twenty years later, for one rea-son or another, I recalled this fellow to Grandmother, repeating his name loudly, for at ninety-five she had developed selective hearing. He's our blood somehow, I shouted, must be.

She considered for a good while and did something between a nod and a sniff. Then she made a pronouncement that renders as well as anything could the kind of logic that goes into the oral tradition.

"Oh yes, I know who you're talkin' about now. He wasn't no relation of ours. He was in trouble *all* the time."

THE WINGED WORM

In the late spring of 1942 I slouched before the sporting goods counter of the general store in New Meadows, Idaho. I was an acolyte in a posture of dreamy, informal worship. Stories had converted me—the stories my father and uncles traded around the kitchen stove.

Home from the woods, they talked with their galluses down, reminiscing about the old homestead in Long Valley forty miles away, where as boys they caught native trout on bent pins. The water, my father would say, sweeping the flat of his hand in a wide circle, was black with them. They fought over the hook. Or, my uncle added with a wink, jumped into your hip pocket.

So I had saved money from my various enterprises—a dollar a week for the lawn in summer, in winter a dime for splitting two days' kindling—until I could stand thus, flush with power, before the oak counter with a glass top. From the jumble of tackle on display I finally picked the most ill-matched outfit imaginable. A casting rod made for bass and pike in eastern lakes; an old-fashioned reel with traveling guide and star drag (a miniature of the kind designed for swordfish); fifty-pound test sturgeon line; gut leader, a book of number eight snelled hooks, and three immense, garish salmon flies.

In my memory now nothing else remains but a huge painting, behind the counter, of Custer's Last Stand, with bursts of fire and smoke from gun muzzles and twisted bodies of horses and men. The storekeeper is gone too, but for his Cheshire Cat expression of mingled mirth, pity, and perhaps a secret satisfaction at having cleared his inventory of so many misfits at once.

THE WINGED WORM

When the snow was almost gone from the mountains behind the mill, the war receded. All winter we had hunted Jerries and Nips with wooden guns, but now it was June and time to fish. Second grade safely under our belts, I and my best friend, Don Adair, dug two cans of fat worms and hiked to Goose Creek on our own. The stream was roaring back in the canyon, milky and nearly out of its banks. The old man had warned me about this situation: it was spawning season; there wouldn't be many but they might be big.

We worked all afternoon, scrambling through willows, catching clothes and our new gear on branches, wading back and forth across the creek in shallows, our pants chill on goosebump legs. Worm after worm grew pale and spongy in the water, disintegrated or was torn from the sharp steel, bumping along the bottom in the current. We plunged on from one hole to the next, shouting encouragement to each other. Already we were into the peculiar, timeless space that fishermen know. Heat and cold, sun and flies, scratches and sprains—they occur at the perimeter of one's mind. In the still center there is only a pure, excruciating alertness.

I stood on the old two-by-twelve plank that jutted over a deep pool. Farm kids had placed it there for a diving board, weighting the end with a heap of sod. The worm was now threaded on one of the yellow-and-red salmon flies—I hoped with this feathered serpent to gain the best of two worlds— and sank quickly. I ignored the small, deceptive tugs caused by the bait tumbling over rocks or submerged roots. At first, in wild anticipation, I had horsed backwards and snapped the leader on such snags. But in the course of the afternoon I had grown sensitive to nuances of shock. Now, all at once, the line tightened, then relaxed, then twitched again. The pull was sharp, purposeful. I reeled in and examined the hook. Bare. I began to shake, but managed to impale one of the four worms I had left.

Careful as a young priest, I repeated my cast, exactly. The writhing pink worm vanished again. Again the quick, hard pull. Something strong and alive signaled through the line. I jerked, and again the hook flashed up, bare and glinting wicked in the sun. I don't know how I breathed, or moved my hands, to thread on the next-to-last worm. I knew I had never before felt such

11

waves of lust and anxiety. This time, however, nothing happened. Unbearable as it was, I had to accept the possibility that I had failed. The fish was suspicious, or perhaps gone.

I tried again, and again. Nothing. Then I cast once more, in despair—a despair that brought relief from the trembling, and a moment of insight. If he struck again, I would do nothing. I would wait, crafty. I would feed him, gain his confidence. One worm remained to me, the chance for a final act of treachery.

He struck. My hands were welded to the pole, my eyes squeezed shut. Somehow I quelled the wild bounding of my heart and did not lash back, though every nerve was howling with the desire to do so. After two hard tugs the line went slack; then came a series of twitches, and I saw that the line was moving through the water, upstream, not rapidly but steadily. Tentative, I leaned back a little. The tip of the rod dipped and the line straightened, taut as a wire. The butt of the rod, braced on my belt buckle, kicked me. I uttered some kind of sound and tried to run backwards. I fell off the board where it met the bank, one leg plunging into the icy water, the other splayed out on the grass.

Back and forth across the pool the line zipped, thrumming with an energy that short-circuited my own nerves. I could not make my hand turn the pitiful crank of the reel. I staggered to my feet and continued to run backwards, raising my arms over my head. Through the dark water now I could see it, a flashing like a broad knife in the sun. I gave a tremendous heave, falling over flat on my back. I heard a slapping in the water, looked and saw the fish, thrashing, bowing its body almost in a circle, seeming to walk on its tail over the pool until it whopped against the bank. With the intense clarity of a dream, I saw the hook separate from its jaw, the line go slack.

On its own momentum the trout went end-over-end and flopped onto the bank. There it lay for a moment, the gill covers flaring to reveal, within, combs the color of liver. I fought through loops of line as the thick, torpedo body flexed and sprang into the air, bounded and twisted laterally through the grass at the very brink. I ran on my knees, my arms wide for the embrace, and fell upon the trout. My nose was buried in mud, and my knees as

well; but in between I had trapped that cold, muscular form. The force of it, squirming in the pit of my stomach, was tremendous, as if I had reversed Jonah and swallowed the whale.

I remained so, the breath sawing in and out of me, elbows clamped against my ribs and fingers hooked in the grass, until the last desperate convulsion. Then I inched aside until I could grasp the fish and half push, half squirt it further away from the bank. Finally, six feet back from the water and wedged between two large stones, the catch was secure enough so that I could actually see it, register it, know what I had done.

The thing was immense. Though perhaps only a third of my length, it was not all sparrow bones and spaces. The body was solid, as big as my leg, and the flesh felt hard as a rubber ball. Its jaws gaped fiercely, and the raked teeth, when I ran a finger along them, felt sharp as my father's coping saw. It was also beautiful. On top, the color of a green olive, with flecks of black ink; underneath, pearly white with just a hint of rose; and along the side, small perfect dots of brilliant blue, amber, yellow, and scarlet.

I did not know it at the time, and did not learn it for many years, but this moment—when the trout's life has flared out, leaving the corpse still glowing, changing color from instant to instant—this is a moment of the highest possible understanding, not merely of the art of angling, but of all human endeavor. It is in this moment that one has the chance to know how the needle of sadness and loss will always invade ecstasy, just at its peak. It is the moment when pursuit turns into triumph; the odd hollow at the crest of exaltation, the dark fear in the back of every hero's mind.

I screamed not for salvation from this awful truth but to summon Don Adair to witness Leviathan.

Don-n-n-n-ee-ee! Don-n-n-ee-EEEE! Lookit!

He burst through the bushes, dead leaves in his hair, sunburned and damp and sullen. One glimpse of his face and I felt myself tipping down a long slide away from the pure and poignant thrill of capture. I jabbered and gesticulated; he wowed and shook his head; we speculated on the dimensions of the fish, all the way up to two feet. But something was wrong, and both of us were quickly subdued. Later in the afternoon he caught his own, smaller but not by much, very respectable. Otherwise, our friendship might not have survived.

The lesson was driven home when we tramped happily back down the highway. A highway, in those days, was a two-lane blacktop usually empty but for the shimmering black pools of mirage. When we passed the Richfield station on the edge of town Mrs. Ross came out onto the concrete, hands on hips, mouth distending. "Floyd!" she hollered. "Floyd come see what these kids got! Lord amighty!" She asked our ages, though she knew them well enough, told us we were fine little men, such fish and only so high. Shy and proud we hoisted the dangling bodies, stiffened now in a partial curl. Floyd emerged from the dark cave of the station, wrench in hand, khaki overalls spotted with grease. He regarded us, his wife yammering away on one side, eviscerated cars and trucks behind him.

"Pretty nice," he grunted. "Goose Creek?"

"Back of Carlock's."

"Worms?"

"Yeah." We waited, yearning to go on and relate everything, just as it had happened, yet held back by some awkwardness of new, sudden growth. We were about to learn more still about the brotherhood of sportsmen, about how the chase can bring us closer, yet make us aware of the chasms of age and life and choice that divide us all.

"Shame you let 'em dry out like that," Floyd said, and turned to stride back into his cave.

17

THE BEAUTICIAN & THE ONE-LEGGED MAN

Weekends the sawmill shut down, and only chuffed an occasional white plume into the blue air to show the boiler was still alive. So Saturday morning, when I got up early to drive Aunt Lucille to the post office, the town was quiet, only a few farm pickups and dogs hanging around the corner store. Nothing seemed out of the ordinary, but as she got out of the car and stepped onto the board sidewalk, she said quickly over her shoulder, "I want to see if there's a letter from my honey."

Then the door slammed and she was striding to the paintless little building where the flag hung limp. Aunt Lucille was the tallest woman in town, thin as a rake, with a horse face and hands and feet as big as a man's. The family word was that a tumor had pressed on her pituitary for a time before going dormant, and she still suffered from terrible migraines. Her gray hair was gathered in a tight bun and she wore one of her straight, plain dresses, this one with shorter sleeves and a loose collar, as a concession to summer.

She nodded at an old rancher exiting the post office with his newspaper and a couple of bills, and he respectfully tipped his hat. Despite the ultimate failure of her two decrepit hotels and the beauty salon, Aunt Lucille commanded respect everywhere, because for a decade she had been justice of the peace, holding court in the hotel lobby. She was the moral conscience of the community, and it was possible to tell, just by the way she inclined her head or shaped her mouth when she examined a miscreant, exactly where he stood in her estimation.

I waited, half stunned, the engine idling. I was trying to grasp all the implications of that word. *My honey!* If we excluded Candy—her ancient cocker spaniel—it was inconceivable that Aunt Lucille would call any creature in the universe by that name. Yet we all knew there had been a time when such a vocabulary must have been possible. On her dresser, cluttered with hair clips, lotions, lacquered boxes, thimbles, crochet hooks, and stale gumdrops in a blue glass bowl, stood a framed picture of a handsome young man in a World War I uniform. In spite of the silly flat-brimmed hat and odd brass buttons, Clyde was not like the people in most old photographs. He looked forthright and strong, with a jaw and brows like the men in the picture shows.

But this sepia image bore no relation to the Clyde who was around for the first eight years of my life, a half-bald man with a gut hanging over his belt buckle and a big nose intricately netted with tiny red and purple veins. In the few minutes I had to myself while Aunt Lucille tarried inside, chatting formally with the postmistress through the iron grillwork, I thought mostly about the last time I had seen him, at the family picnic ten years ago.

We could all tell, even my cousins not yet in school, that there was something strange happening that afternoon. We had spread blankets in a meadow out in Scott Valley near the site of the original family homestead. I sat with the men, stuffed with chicken and potato salad and ice cream, while the women jabbered and clattered dishes, cleaning up. There was my blood uncle who fixed cats and loaders and trucks for the loggers, so he always smelled a little like gasoline and grease; my youngest in-law uncle who was a packer for the Forest Service—a horse smell to him—and my father, who always bore the aroma of yellow pine pitch from the woods. Clyde, I had noticed, smelled like soap and whiskey.

They talked about the old times for a while, bear hunting and building road into the Deadwood mine, and told some well-worn yarns about Grandfather. My father did this well, and related with gusto his favorite, about an old prospector in the Thunder Mountain boom who got an infected toe and was driven by the pain to attempt cutting his own throat, an action he was too weak to perform effectively. My grandfather found him moaning in a pool of blood in his cabin. He patched up this failed suicide and rode on into town in a great huff, filled with profound disgust for such pathetic incompetence. At this and at other anecdotes Clyde laughed long and loud. He sat on the grass, red-faced, saying more than usual. When the bottle came to him, he took it with a trembling reverence.

They moved on finally to business talk, the mysteries of time and money. This confab was sometimes garrulous, sometimes cryptic, all about board feet, mileage, and different prices and makes of saws or boots or wrenches. I knew already that Clyde had bought a new truck, a big rig with a rollaway bed and a chromed stack, and with this truck he was supposed to be hauling posts to North Idaho for use in the mine tunnels. But the trips had been taking longer and longer, and I had overheard my parents talking about that in a tone of disapproval and apprehension. The men betrayed no sign of these feelings but spoke in their flat, matter-of-fact way, with an occasional easy laugh.

At one point the women fell silent and made only a sporadic clanking of dishware, listening intently to the men. Without knowing how I knew, I grasped—not the facts, but the *feeling* they radiated—that the hotels had become the truck, that Aunt Lucille had all her substance riding on those eighteen wheels running north into alien mountains, returning more and more rarely, and that the earnings from the loads of posts were vanishing somewhere, or suspended in repairs or bad debts or taxes.

Clyde, clutching the bottle with his red-faced laugh, was already disappearing from our family; and Aunt Lucille, because of her pride and her judgment, interdicted all comment on the matter, even from Grandmother, and if later all over town there were whispered rumors about the drinking and the Indian girl only twenty years old and the company taking back the truck, I never heard anyone mention Clyde's name again in Lucille's presence. Never, ever. He was effectively deceased, and not until his sudden, resplendent resurrection as "honey" had anyone heard her speak of him. Not for ten years.

But now, around the kitchen table, there was carefully offhand and circumspect reference to the returning prodigal. We were given to understand that he was in a veterans' hospital, had lost a leg because of a clot, but would be released in a few days to hobble home. No one displayed unusual curiosity, as if Clyde had been gone a week instead of a decade. There was merely a polite murmur of regret over the lost limb. Grandmother, however, said nothing. She set her mouth and shuffled with more alacrity during these exchanges, a reaction I interpreted—correctly—as loathing.

My own anticipation was ephemeral, since family matters were inconsequential in my universe, and so were all matters of national security, scientific progress, historical import, and ultimate destiny. Everything, at that time, was peripheral to the question of how far I could get with fifteen-year-old Mary Jo Pugh. At the mill on weekdays, pulling heavy planks of green lumber from the conveyor, I thought about her. Not as a philosopher thinks, in propositions and qualifiers, but as an animal most likely thinks: in abrupt visions of a dug or flank, in a memory of the fascinating scent of newly washed hair, in a general, restive itching, now of the hands, now at the back of the neck, now between the legs. I did not even hear the banshee howl of the saw, the thunder of logs over the deck, the shriek of the carriage powering back and forth. The tremendous gravitational pull of her, or rather something Mary Jo held, as a bottle holds an elixir, kept me in a mental stupor, a glass-eyed addict, except when I was in her presence. Then I was released, a babbling madcap, until the moment in the deep of night when she permitted me to grapple with her on the car seat, and I became nothing more than mindless, squirming, electrified tissues.

But like the purposeful movements of the simplest one-celled beings, who without any brain at all seek darkness, moisture, and warmth, I was squirming nearer a goal, advancing centimeter by centimeter, first along Mary Jo's ribcage until two, then three fingers were hooked under her little breast, and finally along the inner seam of her pedalpushers. When Clyde arrived, at the very end of June, I was well past Mary Jo's knee, and scarcely acknowledged his astonishing transformation.

He had become an old man, bald as a monk, his eyes gone small and

glittery in their craters, his nose now a nearly uniform purple. He propped a torso shapeless as a sack of potatoes on his one good leg and the wooden crutches, his stump waggling inside the empty pantleg folded once and neatly pinned.

"Hello, there, Edwin," he said to me, showing his crooked and tobacco-stained teeth. "By golly."

We began to talk immediately about the mill, his way of saying he knew I was no longer a boy. He asked how many board feet a shift we were stacking off the chain, what the company was paying, and compared that with the dollar a day he had sweated for thirty years ago. Then he made a joke or two about his missing leg—no running after the gals from now on—and that was that. We sat down to lunch, and by some simple, unobtrusive miracle, he was part of the family again, for good.

In the course of those ten years Aunt Lucille had also grown older, but only as a matter of gray hair and deeper lines. She remained ramrod-straight, her large, protuberant eyes as sharp as ever. The hotels, of course, were gone, and finally the beauty salon went, too. For the first few years the place grew merely dingy, curtains fading in the sun, cobwebs in the front windows. A time or two a week, Lucille would open up, dust off the counters, and do somebody's hair. But when once a newcomer to the valley, in a conversation within earshot, asked if that abandoned place—the one that *used* to be a beauty shop—was for rent, it was the end.

Lucille put a sign in the window, took the last of the dryers, a huge, roaring, bubble contraption, and withdrew to her home. There, in a back room, she rigged a short length of hose over a laundry sink, near a shelf devoted to gels, shampoos, combs, and scissors, and there she took care of the handful of elderly customers who perhaps admired and respected her, or perhaps were obscurely intrigued and titillated by her staunch confrontation of her humiliation.

I stayed away when these rare ladies tottered in for an electric hot curl. Lucille's house became then a lair that exhaled a rank and suffocating female decay. Candy waddled about, nearly blind and not in complete control of her bowels, contributing her own ammoniac reek to the dense atmosphere of

burned hair and cheap cologne. At these times the litter of mail-order cata-
logues, old copies of *Redbook* and *Good Housekeeping*, stained coffee cups,
nail files, and plastic grapes was rendered more oppressive than usual, and
Lucille was possessed by a brittle, remote gaiety, concentrated into herself
with a comb clenched in her teeth.

After Clyde's reappearance she summarily cancelled all permanents, and
forestalled all speculation on the oddity and drama of that event with a moral
authority of a new kind: she developed a firm, small smile that radiated
confidence and a justified faith. She had a mysterious power to establish
protocol, and by means of it she inhibited all open talk of what had happened,
quenched all curiosity about those ten years of agony. It was simply:
"Clyde's down at the store," or "He's coming to pick me up at six," or "We'll
be going to Boise this weekend." And the smile.

Clyde drove the old sedan, working a push-rod he had rigged on the
clutch pedal, while she sat bolt upright beside him, giving an occasional nod
or a regal twiddling of fingers to passing friends. At the store she descended
and made her purchases, exchanging small talk with the grocer and other
shoppers, discussing perhaps the Grange plan to collaborate on a benefit
quilt, a square from each of the ladies, or the arrangements for the Old
Timers' picnic to be held on Labor Day. She did everything, in short, as she
had always done it, but now with a detectable contentment, almost a dream-
iness, that awed and silenced the townspeople just as her grim, proud ad-
herence to routine had formerly done. Clyde, for his part, played it easy and
genial, a familiar but less boisterous version of his younger self. He puttered
about the two or three small properties Lucille had managed to retain, directing workmen in the repair of a roof or plumbing, or chatting with the
tenants. I layed sewer pipe for him one weekend, and he seemed content to
sit on a wheelbarrow, smoking and telling me stories. Unlike the rest of the
family he did not query me sharply or stealthily about Mary Jo. He made a
couple of small jokes, the usual stuff about how hard or how many times a
night, but laughed only in a general way and then went on.

At the mill it was often much worse for me. A couple of the old buzzards
in the drying yard would get their talons in my back for the whole lunch hour,

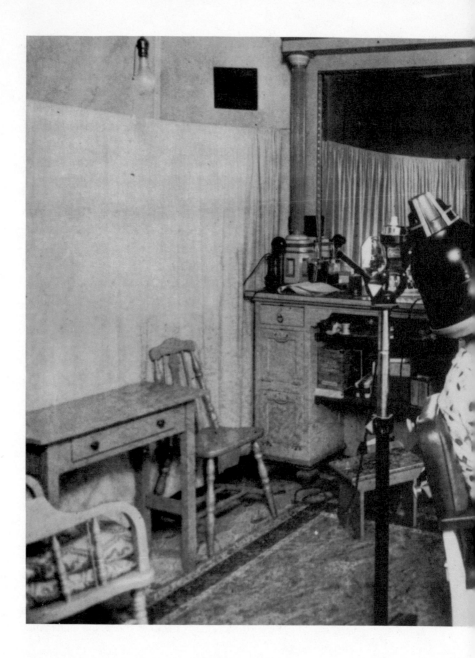

trying to get my temper up by asking me to show my tongue, let them smell my fingers, or stand aside and let a grown man do the job. I could not always cover my embarrassment and occasional murderous anger, and then they would howl with glee. What they did not know, or so I thought, was how I puzzled and dreamed over the mysterious, depraved acts they accused me of either doing or not doing; how I melted at the prospect of some night descending into the magical gloom of Mary Jo's body, of wandering lost in those rank, forbidden thickets, of plunging finally into her darkness.

The excruciating blend of fear, fascination, and overwhelming desire left me alternately exhausted and galvanized with a lunatic energy. I would work eight hours on the chain, and as the day progressed I heaved the great planks out on their cribs with greater and greater ferocity, reaching a near-frenzy in the sultry afternoon. After the whistle, we pulled off our gloves and leather aprons, leaped into the old jalopy that belonged to one of my companions, careened around the leaning stacks of golden lumber to the highway and thence, hunching full-throttle, racketed through meadows of green fire that seemed to be consuming the red and white cattle, through scatterings of jackpine, past sagging rail fences and collapsed barns, to Franky's where we drank illegal beer and shot pool with an intense, arrogant insouciance for an hour. Then it was full-throttle home, where I banged into the bathroom, shed my clothes stiff with sweat and pitch, and slid gasping into a tub of steaming water. I lay there, head propped on the porcelain incline, knees aloft, my hand kneading my balls, which were still knotted with the day's dreams.

By means of muffled shouts through the closed door, interrupted by the dash of my ablutions, I evaded or mocked my parents, whose interrogations had grown intolerably wheedling and aggressive. No they didn't smell any beer on me or if they did it was an old spill in Bill's car. No I hadn't heard about the five teenagers from Boise killed in a head-on. Yeah I was going to the movies with Mary Jo. No I was just washing my hair. Yeah yeah, on my head. Yeah her mother knew and it was OK and no I didn't know when I would be home.

I was dressing in clean blue jeans, polished boots, a crisp white shirt with collar open and cuffs rolled up on my brown wrists, but not too far because my forearms still looked thin to me, despite two summers of hard labor. Yeah we might go somewhere and fool around afterwards. With Bill and Gail maybe. Fool around meant fool around. Talk, drive up to the reservoir, get cokes. I was shaving my upper lip, then a splash of ice-blue lotion on the neck. I said it means what it means what it means. Oh Jesus Christ how do I know. I'm not talking that way to my mother I'm just talking to myself. Oh piss on it!

I slammed the door and ran out of my resentment as one runs out of a cave into the sunlight. I ran to my 1941 Plymouth with one burnt valve, and, peeling rubber nonetheless, made my way via alleys and crossroads to Mary Jo's house. She would watch from the window and bolt down the steps toward me, hoping to outdistance her mother, a thin, fierce woman who sometimes came right after us, waving her cigarette, frowning and admonishing me again that midnight was absolutely by God the limit on a week night, her kid was only fifteen years old, and we had been an hour and ten minutes late last time, while Mary Jo yelled over her shoulder mother, MOTH-er, we're just going riding around for a little to get a coke and not anything else, criminey!

Then, after my ducking and simpering obeisance to maternal commands shouted through a half-open car window, we would wave hypocritically and drive away as fast as we dared, hating everything, absolutely everything behind us, and crazy for what was ahead. I would pull the old car into the weeds overlooking the reservoir shimmering in starlight, and there we would climb out and spread a blanket and hurl ourselves into a tense, nerve-twanging embrace, falling free, together, into an abyss of pleasure until she apprehended my crawling fingers and insistent knee and brought us to a wrenching, agonized halt.

After the sewer pipe we had moved on to rerouting Grandmother's hot water line. One afternoon we cross-threaded a coupling, could not find the dies to recut it, and had to quit. I began packing up the tools and Clyde lurched away from the wheelbarrow with a sigh that I knew intuitively was false.

"Can't do no more now, Edwin," he said. He secured his crutches and balanced on them for a moment, reflective. Across the field the house seemed to slump in the windless heat. Candy lay dead asleep in the shade of the cottonwood tree, and Lucille had gone to Church Auxilliary.

Clyde began to swing his good leg in a rhythmic pendulum arc toward the old Dodge pickup and spoke matter-of-factly over his shoulder. "Throw them tools in the back and let's go on downtown."

But it was Sunday. I knew the hardware and lumber store was closed, and when we passed in front of the Chief Bar Clyde grunted, so I angled in to park. It seemed an accident that old Jeff Purday was just going in, bent nearly double with his arthritis. They gripped each other by the shoulder a little unsteadily, with affectionate curses, and quite naturally we all moved inside where it was cool and dark.

Angus McCulhenny and his Basco sheepherder stood at the far end of the bar, drinking beer, and some fishermen from out of town had a table at the back. Phyllis Haskins sat on a stool near the wash of blue sunlight that came through the tinted and shaded front window. A cigarette bearing a scarlet lip-print slanted in her fingers, and her eyes were magnified behind lenses trimmed with rhinestones.

"Well here we go," she said, and picked up the glass of ice and bourbon before her. "Mr. Clyde Kelly. Jeffrey. Son of a buck. Who's that good lookin' boy?"

I smiled at her perfunctorily.

"Ma'am," said Jeff, bobbing up a little, since he was already in a permanent bow.

"Clyde, Jeff, young feller." Joe, the owner, waited before us. He was a paunchy, poker-faced man who wore a white shirt, winter and summer.

"Let's give Jeff here a beer and we'll keep him company," Clyde said genially and waved in my direction.

30

"Three?" It was not a true question, because he was already moving to pick up the glasses, clinking them together with the fingers of one hand. I was legally too young to drink, and they all knew it, but beyond that they must have known also the real enormity of what we were doing, if Lucille should find it out. I also knew somehow that they would never tell her, and that we would leave in the pickup before she could spot it, returning from the church meeting, and that no one else in town who saw the Dodge parked in front of the Chief would say a word. Here, I knew without knowing how I knew it, was the other side, the dark side, of Aunt Lucille's moral power, the way it created a shield of silence around us now. Behind that shield, vigorous as a wild seed, an easy, natural fellowship took root.

"You back," Joe said, setting out the glasses overflowing with gouts of foam. "Damned if you ain't."

"What's left of me," Clyde said. "Goddamn peg-leg." He raised the glass, nibbled at the foam a moment, smacked his lips and raised the glass higher still. "Ladies and gents."

"Son of a buck," Phyllis said.

By late July there was enough on the landing and in the pond to run the mill six days a week, and the trucks kept dust in the air all over town, rolling through one after another, their beds stacked high with new logs. Tourists were stopping, too, on their way to the high lakes and national forest campgrounds, and some big outfits in the valley were moving cattle to the highest mountain pastures. Rags of snow draped above timberline all summer now vanished, and the hayfields turned golden, ready for mowing. Between Mary Jo and me some things had also turned, shifted, or evaporated, and others had concentrated and intensified. We did not laugh much now, except with others, and took no more idle walks to the drugstore or the river. We talked incessantly or rather I talked and she interrupted out of desperation. I yammered about how I was going away to college, how rarely we would see each other, how we had to make everything count now, how there was only this stupid town to worry about—and look at them, the ones who stayed

31

here, who cared what they thought?—and how we were different from these sad souls.

Then we would clutch again, as if to brace ourselves against a fearsome gale, and collapse awkwardly to the ground or to the old couch on her back porch or into the hay in Billy's parents' barn loft, and there we would remain, arms and legs moving in slow but frantic gestures, like heavy sea creatures unexpectedly aground. By this time, early August, I could regularly unhook her brassiere and clamp a palm over one breast, and the fingers of the other hand had attained their goal, or very near it, only to discover that the tiny chapel was barely detectable behind a gate of iron-tough denim. Often I cursed the evolutionary fate that provided me with only two hands, for artfully as I might shift them, Mary Jo always knew by some infallible divination how to intercept them or squirm under them in a fashion that both evaded and invited, until my nerves shuddered with yearning and exhaustion.

The battle line was now at the second button of her jeans, where a small wedge of tender flesh, cream-white below her tanned midsection, emerged between the flaps of the fly. Then, one afternoon in the hayloft, I managed to slide a finger under the hem of her panties, and she burst into tears, twisting away from me.

"That's all you ever want," she said with a sharp sob, "stick your old hand in there just as soon as I hardly set down."

"Hey, wait," I protested weakly, fighting out of my sensual trance. "What's the deal? All of a sudden? Hey, sweetheart." I slid one hand again down her back. "Last week . . ."

"My mom said to keep my pants on, no matter what, because you're eighteen and that's all they want, and I guess she sure is right."

She pushed herself up on her knees, bits of straw on her blouse and in her tousled hair. She began to fumble with the top buttons and I caught her hands.

"Baby," I said intently, "listen." But I really had no idea what incantation would stop her from sealing up that precious wedge of skin. "Listen to me."

"Well?" She stared at me, resentful, the tear tracks bright on her cheeks.

"Don't cry," I said stupidly, and then came a burst of inspiration. "How does your mom know? What was she doing when she was this age? You know?" I released her hands and made a gesture of confident dismissal.

Mary Jo looked uncertain. "She never. Not when she was my age. She had me when she was nineteen."

"So? Then she had to get pregnant when she was eighteen. And you don't just start in doing it and bang you're knocked up, do you?"

"Well, you could."

"Huh uh. No sir. Bill tried to breed Rio to Cartwright's mare, and it took him six months. And that's *horses*. So what were they doing when they were seventeen? Your folks? Or sixteen? A lot worse than this, you bet."

"I'm not sixteen," she said sulkily, but she was no longer tugging at her buttons.

"Two months."

"Anyway, if she knew—"

"She doesn't. Nobody does, except Billy and Gail. And we're not *doing* anything. I mean, you can't get pregnant just *touching* somebody."

She sniffled. "You can get pregnant from lots of things. From toilet seats."

"Oh come on, Mary Jo. That's just bull hocky. Anyway," I made a comical face, "do I look like a toilet seat?"

She laughed then through the sniffles.

"Look." I shifted suddenly to my rakish and tormented James Dean expression. "I mean I really *want* to. I can't help it. When we kiss that way, I just . . ." I looked down to hide my suffering, picked up a straw and stared at it in bitter hopelessness. ". . . I go crazy."

Moments passed. "Oh shoot, I know," she whispered finally, and walking on her knees she came to me and buried her face in my collar bone. "I know I know, I want to too, but you just can't you know because if that happens . . ."

"I know I know." I slid my hand again down her back, to the belt line of her jeans.

33

"And you keep after me so much, it's like I just can't ever . . ." She hiccupped a final sob.

"I know I know." I breathed deeply through the net of her hair. "I can't help it."

We fell over together in the straw, and at dusk she undid the second button herself. The tips of all four fingers were inside the hem and I had the rare craftiness to pause there, leisurely, masterful, triumphant, stroking very gently the first, few tiny curls, while Mary Jo uttered long, trembling sighs of fear and ecstasy.

The week before Labor Day Aunt Lucille began to clean house, a top-to-bottom cleaning, perhaps for the first time in a decade. I hauled away boxes of junk: old clothes, coathangers, empty bottles of shampoo or cologne, a ruptured mattress, worn-out tires and magazines that smelled like mold when I leafed through to see the peculiar automobiles and hair styles of another era. Except for a mahogany cane which I calculated was Grandfather's and therefore worth preserving, there was nothing of any value to me except these old images from the past, from between the great wars.

People looked absurd then, clothes plastered tightly to emaciated bodies, moustaches and eyebrows pencil-thin, eyes huge and predatory above cheeks feverish with rouge. It was impossible to imagine my parents or Lucille and Clyde as contemporaries of these brightly painted dolls who propped themselves elegantly against square Buicks and Packards, smoking Chesterfields. In the family albums, in fact, my relatives seemed largely unchanged by youth. They stood dirty and gaunt in workclothes before ancient rakes and binders or farmhouses already dilapidated and paintless. The occasional fancy portraits seemed posed by strangers, awkward in dark, stiff clothes and lacquered coiffures, savages who bore little resemblance to that race of Egyptian royalty in the magazines. At first I kept back one or two issues to show Mary Jo, but it was also impossible to imagine these creatures without clothes in a hayloft—a troubling dimension of their sophistication. So I threw away the whole batch, gloriously relieved to be alive now, the sun hot on my bare, brown back as I stood in the bed of the Dodge and hurled box after box out the back, pages fluttering like birds shot out of the sky.

When I returned to the house, the silent Japanese woman had departed with her scrub bucket, leaving the kitchen linoleum gleaming. She and Lucille had vacuumed the rugs, washed the curtains, and polished the furniture. A neighbor boy was just finishing the lawn and lilac bushes. Grandmother had arrived to fry the chicken, her specialty, since the next day all our kin would gather for the Old Timer's picnic. She was shuffling around in the kitchen, and probably for that reason Clyde was out back, poking with the rubber tip of a crutch in the last load of refuse I was to haul. He seemed preoccupied and motioned peremptorily for me to back up to the heap. His face under the old hat was flushed and sweating and there were damp patches on his khaki workshirt, freshly ironed that morning.

"What part of Asia you been to?" he asked when I descended to begin heaving in the empty oil cans, broken springs, and rusted parts cleaned out of the garage. "Never mind. Let's git this load out. Lucille's down with a headache and I'm tired of fiddle-fartin' around." He stumped around the tailgate and peered into the bed. "That old tractor seat, Edwin, belonged to the Case I had when we built the Warm Lake road. I was a young feller then and I could damn near lift the front end of that tractor by myself."

"I was lookin' at the magazines," I explained. "I got interested."

"Well." He thought a moment. "Git a good education." He jerked his head at the distant sawmill. "You don't want to ride a damn green chain your whole life."

I lifted in the last crate and banged the tailgate closed, hooking the drop-chains to hold it. "I ain't goin' to," I said, and I meant it.

He swung himself to the cab, opened the door, and unhinged himself from the crutches, which he stacked inside. "I'm goin' with you. Got to stop and see a feller on the way back."

"At the Chief." I smiled.

"Now Edwin." With his arms he jacked himself up on the seat and then, using both hands, hoisted in his good leg.

I climbed in beside him, loose and lean and quick, and we both laughed, for no reason, when the engine coughed and roared to life.

I consumed four bottles of beer at the Chief, didn't go home, picked up Mary Jo and that night, on a blanket under the stars, sank my middle finger in her to the hilt. Her alarm and excitement were such that she put a hand on me, so some tremendous circuit was completed. Time was annihilated, and benumbed in our transport, we did not return from the reservoir until three in the morning. The next day, in a tense, small-voiced telephone conversation, Mary Jo told me her mother had had a fit and had forbidden us to go out again, not even to the community dance to be held in the Oddfellows Hall after the picnic. Also she was afraid she might get pregnant from my finger, if I had been touching myself, doing that thing. I lied and said I hadn't.

My own parents were only grim and watchful. In two weeks I would be leaving for college and they doubtless hoped that disaster might be avoided if they did nothing erratic. I was myself in the grip of an accelerating, desperate melancholy. Every fiber in my being was now concentrated on reconnection with Mary Jo, on the perpetuation of that awesome current that had riveted us together for so many hours. I knew that another night or two would bring me to those ultimate unspeakable acts, the final, explosive release of a beast that had been prodded and teased in its cage for months, reduced finally to one long, continuous, insane howl of desire. I pictured the two of us over and over, writhing like serpents, our kisses blossoming swiftly into new visions of breathtaking lewdness, visions I had never before permitted myself.

So we had agreed to find ourselves at Franky's, separately and as if by accident, before the dance. This rendezvous was another dangerous step; although Franky did not check identification rigorously for mill hands, Mary Jo was far too young to pretend. Even if she sat at the grill and drank coke, word might get back to her mother. With its jukebox, pool table, and occasional fistfights, Franky's was not a fit place for young ladies under eighteen, and I wondered at Mary Jo's sudden, calm fatalism in agreeing to meet there.

Our family picnic was for me a blurred dream, an interminable confusion of paper plates, giggling cousins, and repetitious jokes—idle teasing about my ungainliness, my shaven upper lip, my "gal." Despite the wretched frustration of having to smile at these sallies, I noted certain details over the afternoon. I saw the bottle in the paper sack between the knees of my packer uncle, saw Grandmother sitting alone in the portable lawn chair, staring bleakly at the mountains, saw Lucille touching her brow distractedly, grimacing a brave smile, and heard Clyde laugh, loud and taut, as he had on that other afternoon many years ago.

The children seemed frenetic and irritable, galloping in and out of the clearing where card tables were set up, and when one of them, before dessert, stepped in a nest of yellowjackets, I seized the opportunity to hitch a ride into town. My mechanic uncle drove as fast as he dared on the gravel road and I rode in the back with the whimpering boy, his eyes already swollen shut.

After they dropped me off I walked to the slough behind the mill and began to kill time, throwing stones at floating cans and bottles. The aspens had turned and the new gold was striking against hills gone a dusty, dull green over the summer. In the hot, blue sky a few cottony clouds were moored and a hawk hung motionless among them. I threw harder and harder, rifling the rocks into the water with a sound like the sudden tearing of heavy canvas. It was only two hours before my tryst with Mary Jo, but the sun seemed nailed to the sky, the shadows painted to the ground.

My mind was strangely empty, even of the wild and tangled visions of desire. I felt more anxiety than anticipation, and wanted only to break bottle after bottle after bottle. I did not know where my savagery came from, except the summer was nearly over, and I knew suddenly that more than anything I wanted it to be over—no more arguing with my parents, no more pitch and sweat and dirty jokes from cretins at the mill, no more of this

shabby town hemmed in by mountains, and no more of its grotesque, ignorant inhabitants. At college there would be young, clean, glamorous people—scientists and artists and athletes—who spoke foreign languages,
dressed and moved in marvelous ways, like the people in the magazines
from another age. There was nothing I wanted here. Everything that mat-
tered was there, in the future. Everything except Mary Jo.

It was all at once sundown and I fled home, to discover the Plymouth had
a dead battery. I took my old bicycle and in the soft, luminous dusk I pumped
down the highway, which still exuded a hot, tar breath, through the empty
hayfields, now only stubble, past the ruined barns, to Franky's. I was sweating and my knees were trembling when I leaned the bike against the corner
of the building. The gravel parking lot was almost full of cars and pickups,
and the regular thud from the juke box made the plate glass of the windows
shiver slightly.

Inside I saw the booths in the soda fountain and grill section were mostly
full, and the bar, more dimly lit, was crowded too. I took a step toward the
booths, but already I could see they were occupied by mothers and fathers
and children hunched over their hamburgers. Mary Jo was nowhere in sight.
Then a voice hailed me from the bar and I saw a group from the mill. Their
faces were clean-shaven, their pearl button shirts fresh and bright. With
special heartiness they clapped me on the back, wondered at the sweat still
on my brow, and ordered me a beer.

I stood with them at the bar, where we were jammed shoulder to shoulder. Cowboys from up and down the valley, mill hands, and loggers were
fueling themselves for the dance, which, as it was sponsored by the Eastern
Star and held in the Odd Fellows Hall, would not permit the sale of spirits.
There were booths at the back here, too, and in the tiny floor space before
the juke box a few couples were already gyrating and swaying.

"Goin' to the shindig tonight?" someone shouted to me over the din. I
shrugged and drank from the bottle to show my lack of concern.

"You got to run down that little gal first," said one of the older men,
squinting his eyes slyly. He glanced around toward the juke box, and the

others looked too. When I turned then I saw Mary Jo was there, dancing with a ranch hand. He was from Round Valley, a thin, tall, sour-faced youth named Mel. Watching his own polished boot toes intently, he moved one arm in a stiff, pumping gesture, while with the other he pressed Mary Jo to him, awkwardly but firmly.

Some expression froze on my face before I could control it and the others laughed.

"She's sure kickin' up her heels. You better get a rope on her, buddy."

"Hell, I'll take care of it," someone else put in, and they all laughed again, watching me, but I had turned my back and tipped up the bottle again to hide the shock.

"Goddamn," I said, and smacked my lips in false heartiness, "that tastes good."

The song ended in a long, sad, sweep of steel guitar, and when I looked Mel had bent Mary Jo almost parallel to the floor, her back arching over his cradling arm. There was a smatter of applause and a drunken whoop. Then they righted themselves and people moved around to sit at tables or approach the bar.

Through the milling figures I kept sight of Mary Jo's face, at once gay and furtive. I knew she was looking for me, and when our eyes met the whole room seemed to tilt under my feet. She smiled, then flushed. I stood a little away from the bar, my back rigid. I was conscious of smiling, but it must have been a smile thin and bitter as a winter wind, for after long seconds she looked away, her face aflame. I rocked on my feet, wanting with all my heart to take a step, move across the room to her side, but I could not.

The juke box thudded again. It was the song about Nothin' in the World like a Big-Eyed Girl, and a couple came out on the floor doing the new step we called the Dirty Boogie. Mary Jo stood lame on one foot, looking for an instant like a child, and then Mel had her hand again. She flashed me one desperate glance, then shook her head and laughed, as if for the first time that night. Before I turned away again I saw that she wore earrings and had done something to her hair to make herself older.

My head felt swollen, and the long bar before me appeared unnatural. I stared stupidly at the fuming ash trays, crumpled bills, and ringing glasses, at the brown hands moving like crabs among them. I could scarcely bear to look at the faces thrust near mine, creased sharply in malice and mirth. I spoke with no idea of what I was saying, laughed mindlessly, drank whatever came to hand.

Finally the crowd began to thin. Headlights glared outside and tires spun in the gravel, accompanied by shouts and laughter. People were moving on to the dance. Mary Jo stood near a table of Round Valley people, talking animatedly. She patted her hair, turned and walked toward the restrooms. I pushed away from the bar and angled to intercept her.

"Look who's here," she said with a terrible brightness.

I could feel the millhands behind us watching, and the people at the table she had left openly stared our way.

"Well," I said.

"Well what?"

"Having a good time?" My voice was small, almost choked, and contained a tremor that, when I heard it, filled me with panic and disgust. I rushed on.

"Yeah, I can see you're having a real good time. You bet. Don't let me interfere with your big time."

"What is the matter with you?" Her mouth twisted a little, as if she were going to cry, but the twist became a sneer.

"I'm just fine, just fine. Real good. Don't let me get in the way. Just forget it."

"You're going away to your big college. You don't care. You just wanted one thing, we know what." She took a single, shuddering breath and then lifted her head, defiant, her eyes ready to spill tears. "And you're not the only guy in the whole world, mister."

"Fine, fine," I was backing away, nodding, my face working in a horrible grimace of affability. "Have a big time at the dance with your boyfriend."

She looked stricken. Her face worked for a moment and then she, too, drew back.

"I will. You just bet I will."

I stalked across the floor then, shouldering through the crowd, and

41

plunged out into the night. I wrenched my bicycle away from the building, my face burning with humiliation, thinking absurdly that they were watching through the window, mocking me for having only this child's machine to carry me off. In a fury I pedaled out of the lot and down the highway, driving for home with every ounce of my strength.

The night was cooler on my brow, and the frogs in the marsh were raucous, even louder than the explosions of my own breath. I eased my pace, found a rhythm; the dynamo of rage and shame powering my nerves and muscles began to fail, to convert imperceptibly into a current of careless arrogance, of reckless self-satisfaction. I coasted on a slight grade into town, two fingers loosely on the handlebar, head thrown back to drink the wind.

She was not the only girl in the world either. The way she had snapped her fingers at our private, forbidden pleasure and hurled herself into a cheap honkytonk showed how trivial she was in the first place. Maybe I would go to the dance after all. Yes. Get drunk. Sally Rinker might be there. Sally Rinker, a black-headed little beauty two years behind me in school. With grim daring I smiled to myself in the darkness.

Then, passing Clyde and Lucille's street, I saw lights on and the front door open. Something moved on the walk, a shapeless thing I first thought might be a giant raccoon or even a bear. Warily I circled back and coasted up the driveway. Now the crawling thing had reached the pool of light on the porch and I could see it was Clyde, dragging only one of his crutches. He was swearing, not in a loud voice, but I had never heard swearing like that. He didn't hear the bike tires whisper in the dust, but when I spoke he had reached the stoop where he propped himself to turn and look at me.

A cloud of gnats and a few moths fluttered around the bulb of the porch-light, casting faint, wavering shadows, but I could see his face was the color of old brick, glistening with sweat. Bits of leaf clung to his shirt front and his trouser leg was soiled.

"It's a sight, ain't it," he went on. "I'm the entertainment for the goddamn county, ain't I. Goddamn sonofabitch, Edwin, a man take so much and no more. Your Aunt Lucille went to the goddamn hospital, and her mother, goddamn her—I say goddamn that woman—Edwin, Lucille, she can't walk nor talk . . ." His arms gave way with the strain and he slid, sprawled against the steps. "Goddamn bastard of a fuckin' leg."

I had parked the bike against a tree and had come close enough to smell that he was drunk and to see that he was crying, eyes red and winking out tears, breath coming in short, hacking gasps. He pawed futilely with the crutch, trying to get erect, so I came to him and helped him to his feet. He went on with his tirade, as we lurched through the door into the living room. I gathered that Lucille had fainted at the picnic and had been taken to the county hospital, thirty miles away, that Clyde had returned after a somber consultation with the doctors, had made his own way to the Chief and then to Grandmother's, where she first agreed to serve him a plate of cold chicken but then, when he fell off his chair in the kitchen, refused to help him up. Flailing about in a rage, he had broken one of the crutches against the stove. Still Grandmother refused to help, to lend her cane or her shoulder, had ordered him out of her house. He had had to crawl like a goddamned alligator through the back yard, across empty lots and sidewalks to his own place.

"She don't have no heart, Edwin. Not a goddamn sign nowheres, not the milk o' human kindness as your goddamn poets say. Your own grandmama, now, I hate to say it." He had collapsed on his bed, face squashed flat on one side against the coverlet, and his speech was slurring into hiccups and snores.

I left him there, the lights on, shutting the front door behind me, and walked to Grandmother's. He light was on, too, and when I rapped on the back door she uttered her little croak that meant all right, come on in. She was sitting in her rocker in the living room, commanding a view of the kitchen where I could see the chair still tipped over and the broken crutch. On the table, covered in blue oilcloth, was the forlorn plate, containing a half-eaten drumstick and a dollop of cole slaw.

"Clyde done that," she said when I stopped in front of her. "You see what he done."

She rocked a little, then looked up at me.

"You hungry for some chicken?"

"No."

"He come in here drunk, and I ought to have sent him off, right then, but on account of Lucille bein' took so bad, I fixed him something. He was so drunk, he—"

"I know, Grandmama. I heard."

She pushed with the square toes of her old lady shoes, and the rocker creaked.

"Thrashin' around like a stuck hog. He wasn't never worth nothin'. Wasn't fit to wipe her boots. He ruint her and now she . . ." Grandmother's voice took on a strange tremolo, and her face, withered and lined as the last winter apple on a tree, contracted, pinched inward.

"Now Grandma," I said, and raised one hand nervously.

"She's dyin'. My baby's dyin'."

It was so incongruous to think of Aunt Lucille as a baby that I shook my head with an idiotic laugh.

"She'll be all right, Grandma."

"That man," she said, barely audible now. "There's no use to him. No use at all." She stopped rocking abruptly and looked at me.

"Edwin, you know better. You go on to school and get yourself an education. And you be careful with that girl. That Pugh girl."

"I am, Grandma."

"You do right by that girl."

I raised my hand again, as if to swear. "I *am*, Grandma."

"Now you go on home. Your folks are still down to the hospital, but they'll want to know where you are. We all got to go back tomorrow and talk to the doctors, and see her. She don't recognize nobody, though. Not her own mother." She pushed the rocker into motion again.

I could think of nothing to say, so I left, looking back in the doorway to see her staring into the darkened room.

Lucille died after a week in a coma, the tumor having become demonic. Already gone to enroll in college, I missed the funeral. When I came back at

Christmas, Clyde had progressed from beer to whiskey, and was back in the VA hospital for treatment. One weekend in the spring I hitched a ride home, and mother mentioned that he was in a rest home near the hospital, and since his own kin were all gone or didn't care, and none of ours would go, she thought we might pay him a visit. She hinted he didn't have long. A pitiful thing.

We found him in a sunny corner of a big room, in a wheelchair. The others who peered and gibbered at us as we made our way to him were in white smocks or bathrobes, but Clyde wore his construction man's khakis still, though these fitted him poorly now. His torso had shrunken, and the bulbous nose was incongruous as a clown's in a face now hollowing into a skull. He brightened when we approached, an expression of confused, desperate delight.

"Now, now," he said, "look here. How's it going, mama, young feller? What are you sawin' down to the mill?"

I shook his hand, the soft knobs of his fingers barely contracting, like a baby's. "I'm in school, now, Clyde. In college."

"Now, now," he said and looked at mother. "What about that, mama? An education in college. That's mighty fine. I never did, no sir. But I burnt the paint off the first cat they ever run in the Blue Devil mine. Damn it if I didn't."

He proceeded to tell such stories, garrulous and disconnected, interrupting himself sometimes to complain about the food or the smell of the old goofs who surrounded him. Mother and I smiled blankly and told him a little harmless news, and squirmed in our chairs.

Once he said, "How's that little galfriend of yours, Edwin? That cute little gal?"

"Well," I answered lamely, "not too good."

Mother gave a puffy little sigh. *"That."*

"She's gonna marry some guy from Round Valley," I added shortly. "Okay by me."

"You be careful," Clyde said and raised one of his knobby fingers with a death's head leer. "These little gals." He shook his head. "Now Lucille and I

45

we been married fifty years, damn near, excuse me mama, and there ain't a finer woman walks the earth. No sir. Damned if there ain't. God never made one." He looked out the window to the yard in the sun, where a few of the hunched men in smocks stood like ruined columns. "You never seen her comin' in?"

Mother and I looked at each other.

"Well," he uttered an easy, deprecating laugh, his familiar charm, "she's down to the post office, I circumspect. She'll be back before long."

He rambled on a while longer and then a nurse came through to ask if we were staying for dinner, because it was soon time. We said no and got up quick and made our goodbyes.

I didn't want to look back and neither of us said much until we were in the car and moving away.

"I feel sorry for him," mother said when she had reached high gear. "He's a poor creature. It's so sad to see somebody like that."

"Uh huh." I was watching the storefronts passing by, the people walking along, thinking about how indescribably awful it would be to have to sit at a long table and eat, every day, beside those wrinkled, drooling wretches. My heart was lifting from a sentimental sadness into a tremendous, secret joy that I was who I was, where I was.

"But he brought it on himself." Mother glanced at me and her hand flexed on the steering wheel. "He surely did."

She drove in silence for a while and then she expelled another small, emphatic sigh and said, more to herself than to me, "And to think he used to be such a *handsome* man."

THE NEARDEATH OF AUNT NELLIE

I

Jess didn't meet the plane, so I sweltered at bus stops in the Tucson sun. Eventually (wondering if she died as I crawled through Saturday traffic), I got to the hospital, to the white bed.

Her features, under rudely chopped gray hair, had withered. Her flesh appeared to have sunk inward, and her arms were blackened and swollen. A tube hung out of one of them, connecting her to a hanging bottle.

She hoisted herself out of the pain to talk.

"Jess needs y' so much, Edwin. Y' don't know how much he needs y'."

"I had to see you too, Nellie."

"I know y' do, honey. Phyllis 'n Ollie Mae was 'sposed to be here and Jess can't find where they's at. Will you please hep 'im, honey?"

Jess said, "I know damn good 'n well they come in. Had to. I ask that ape out at the airport and he said they was on the plane. I dunno where the hell they went." He shook his head and looked down, then up quickly, his moustache sharp and his blue eyes wide and wet. "Goddamned if I do."

I went to work on the phone, but while I was cajoling a ticket agent into checking passenger lists, Phyllis and Ollie Mae walked in.

"Oh my God. You'ns."

"Don't talk, honey."

"We been here since . . . When'd we git here, Phyllis?

"We had you paged, Jess."

49

"I dinged around there thinkin' you'd be along to get your bags 'n then went and had coffee . . ."

"Hello, Edwin."

"Stayed all night in Boise on account of Earl had to go down Friday anyway for *his* tests."

"How is Earl?"

"I got a story to tell you'ns." Nellie lurched forward away from the propped-up bed. "They was these two lions always went around together, huntin' together and all. But this time the huntin' wasn't so good so they went into town and they was a bar 'n grill there so in they went 'n set down 'n the waitress come and the first lion he ordered a big steak. The second lion's alookin' over at the bar an' the first lion says what's the matter with you, dontya want somethin' to eat? Second lion nods towards the bar an' says lookathat. There was a blonde asittin' there, just the most beautiful thing he ever saw. That there's what *I* want, the lion says. Better git a steak, the other lion, the first one, says. She sure won't agree with you. But the second lion he gits up and goes in the bar just aswitchin' his tail like this and lickin' his chops 'n he comes up behind this beautiful blonde, most beautiful thing he ever seen, and pops her in his mouth and just gobbles her up, red dress 'n all. M-m-m M-m-m, he says, best thing I ever had. Well the other lion just growls and finishes his steak and then they go home. Next day, the first lion, one had the steak, he gits up 'n goes down to the corner to meet his friend and go huntin' like always. But the second lion don't show up an' he don't show up an' he don't show up, and finally the first lion gets worried so he goes over to the other lion's cave and inside he can hear that lion agroanin' and moanin'. 'Oh-h-h my God! Oh-h-h-h Jesus my head!' 'What the hell's the matter with you?' 'I'm so loggy I can't git up; my head's swole up big as a bushel basket.' So the first lion says, 'Why goddamn you, you old fool, I tried my best to warn you away from that bar bitch you ate.'"

Nellie fell back in bed, showing her gums and wheezing.

Ollie Mae put her hand over her mouth and bent over in her chair.

"Oh shit Nellie," Phyllis jumped. "Bar-bitch-ur-ate. Oh shit."

Jess grinned through his pain. I laughed. Nellie threw up, and we all hurried clumsily to blot it with tissues and get the crescent-shaped stainless steel pan to her lips to catch the rest of it. After a while nurses came and drew white curtains around her and we had to leave.

Jess and I wandered around the hospital grounds. A few scrubby trees were scattered over the lawns, and decorative cacti grew along the low adobe wards, all named after Indian tribes: Apache, Papago, Moqui, Navajo. We sat under a tree and talked.

"By God Cochise held 'em off up there. Can't see from here, goddam smog, but there's a group of little crags at one end of that range there—call 'em the Dragoons—and there's springs in there in the rocks only he knew about. If they hadn't run low on cartridges he'd be there yet. I tell you. The white man, supposed to be civilized, spoiled every goddamned thing he ever got aholt of. We come along and butchered all the game and pissed in the streams and cut down all the trees. Hell yes they fought back, anybody would. Just like the Vietnamese. Fight for their homes and we call that 'n act of aggression. I tell you, Ed, what I think oughta be done."

"What?"

"They oughta take those cocksuckers in Washington out here in the desert and break both their ankles and let 'em crawl home. An' bomb the piss outa 'em all the way."

"Yeah."

Jess sighed and gripped his temples with one hand, grimacing and kneading his contorted brows. "I don't understand how a people supposed to be civilized can do that. Why goddamn it the wolves has got sense enough not to kill any more than they can use. You know I used to think it was just the economic system that was founded on the exploitation of the worker, but by God I've come to wonder . . ." His blank, steel eyes were watering. "I've thought and thought about how many jillions of years ago the first creature swum up out of the mud. You ask yourself, 'Does the bird fly because he's got wings or does he got wings because he needs to fly? Does a man think because he has a brain or does he have a brain on account of he thinks?'

Highly developed, I mean. It all goes back to a first cause. If man could just get a line on that, he might get somewhere. But goddamn Socrates and all the philosophers of the world has tried and tried for generations and there's not one of 'em ever got to it. Oh, some got closer'n others, but you know."

"Yeah. I know."

"That first cause, they know there must be one, got to be, but they only know it was some kind of explosion, sendin' out whirlin' gases."

"Yeah."

"I've worked on the internal combustion engine all my life, and I know: if the air and fuel and spark all hit together and there's compression, why she's bound to take off. There's life."

"Yep."

"But that first compression stroke. We don't have no more idea than a pissant where it come from. Do we?"

"Nope."

We reflected for a time. Convalescents and their families chatted under other trees.

A pretty young nurse was approaching. I tried to wrap up the conversation.

"Well, Jess, people die. Nobody figures out why."

"We're all through now."

"Thank you honey. You sure are lookin' fine today. I'll be right along. That's true. But goddamn it we ought to know better, shouldn't we? After three thousand years, since the dawn of civilization? You comin'?"

"Nope. I want to talk to that doctor in about five minutes."

He nodded, and rose by ramming both hard and horny fists into the grass. The nurse ahead of him, they left the pool of shade under the tree and crossed the hot, brilliant courtyard. Jess did not look back.

II

"You are Mrs. Baker's _____?"

"Nephew."

Doctor Fine was tall, freckled, and cool. "Yes. Well. Your aunt is dying of

carcinoma of the liver—cancer—and we don't know how long she will be with us. We'll make her comfortable. This was a very strong drug. It was a chance she agreed to take. Of course we're keeping a close check on her. If there is any change . . ."

He was rocking on one long leg, twiddling his stethoscope, wanting loose.

"When will you know the results of the brain scan and . . ."

"I believe that is scheduled for this afternoon."

"She had it this morning."

"Oh. Yes. Well, so tomorrow . . ."

"I guess the drug didn't take effect."

"It may have inhibited the progress of the parent cancer. We don't know. But there was not much hope of recovery, you understand, at any time."

"Yeah. I understand."

I went back to Nellie's ward. Phyllis and Ollie Mae and Jess were sitting in the lobby talking and smoking.

"She's awful low, Edwin."

"You figure it's that drug?"

"Doctor says so."

"Does he know what he's talkin' about?"

"How can you tell? They never say anything."

"Ed, she hasn't eat for twenty days." Jess kept pulling at his white moustache. He had it honed to two points, swept up like miniature long-horns. "Goddamn it."

"You folks go get coffee. I'll sit awhile."

"I can't leave 'er Ed." He made a snorting sound.

"Get out of here, Jess. You're not doin' any good."

"I know. But goddamn it."

They left, and I went into the room. She was grayer and they had changed the bottle and tube to her other arm, which was now twice normal size and mottled in blacks and purples.

We exchanged greetings. Then she looked right at me and said, "Did you bring it?"

I was hoping she had forgotten. A month before, they had phoned me in

California to say, indirectly, that I had better come soon, for the last time, while Nellie was still at home. There we could play pinochle and have a few drinks and tell some jokes. She had said then, voice still strong and randy through the wires, "You bring some o' that stuff you'ns talk about. Bring me a marijuana cigarette. I wanta try it by God. Tried everything else." I had promised. But I hadn't done it. Now I started an explanation, but she lost interest. Then her convulsions came back. She sat up to vomit every few minutes, her head nodding over long strings of drool that collected in the steel pan with gobs of chocolate blood. Occasionally she mumbled something.

Phyllis and Ollie Mae came back and we all told her to save her strength. Finally she lay back quietly, her eyes very red and slow to shift.

A younger, brisker doctor entered.

"Well, hello there, Mrs. Baker. How are you today. Now I want you to watch my finger here." He leaned over the bed and extended his index finger to within a foot and a half of her nose. Then he moved it in an arc to her right side. "Watch my finger, Mrs. Baker." He waved it again before her eyes, and moved it again ninety degrees to the right. "Follow my finger." Nellie's red eyes slid a little to the left, meeting mine, and returned to center position. "Come on Mrs. Baker." He moved to the left. "Mrs. Baker, please look at my finger. You must help us to help you, you know."

Nellie's tongue appeared suddenly, like a white mushroom. We laughed, and the doctor glanced around apprehensively.

She reached up slowly and put her finger very lightly on the end of his nose.

"I'm sorry I did that," she said.

III

The trailer house in Wilcox was fixed up nice. They had nursed four elm trees out of the alkali for shade, and added on a room at the back for Jess's tools and an extra bed. Rows and rows of jars full of Nellie's bright green pickles were there too. The four of us sat around the kitchen table, the coffee perker between us, and talked a long time, about medicine, relatives, the Kennedys, Negroes, and the cats, who walked through from time to time. Jess went outside, and after a while Phyllis said something so I went out to look. There wasn't much of a moon, but I could see my way through the scrub and piles of boards and fencing. I ran into him on a bit of road along the back of his property. He was just standing there in the soft dust looking up, kneading his brows.

"First cause. First cause."

"Yeah."

"If a man could get to that . . . Y' know I cannot believe that this is the only planet with intelligent beings. Look at those jillions of stars. It don't stand to reason. That this little speck of dirt is the only place, out of all those jillions and jillions of possibilities, that produced life, just don't stand to reason, Ed. And all was contained in the first cause. Alongside that—"

"Jess . . ."

"Yeah. I know it's self-pity. I'm apityin' myself. She's gonna be all right, one way or the other. But goddamn it, Ed."

I wanted to change the subject.

"How long you guys been married?"

"Forty-two years." He expelled a big breath. "Forty-two years and eight months." We were silent for quite a while. Then Jess tilted his head way back and stared up at the frozen swarms of stars, as if he were reading. When he spoke again his voice was calm, and just barely audible.

"Some of those sonsofbitches, Ed, they ain't even there anymore. Just light. Just plain light."

"Yeah."

The next day a catheter went in, and they had to cut open a fat, purple arm to find a piece of vein to stick the IV tube into. Nellie's retching weakened into a sort of gagging, splattery cough, and she didn't sit up or talk any more. But once, when a nurse came in and called her by the wrong name, I tried to make a joke.

"Hey," I said, "Isn't your name Betty Grable?"

At first I couldn't tell—thought it might be silent laughter—but then, the way she caught her breath, I knew she was crying. I felt the worst I had felt since I got there. She lifted up her arms and pulled me down to her.

"No. No. No, honey. I didn't mean to make you cry. I wouldn't give ten thousand of those movie stars for you. You know I wouldn't."

"Oh Edwin," she whispered. "I smell so bad. I know I do smell just awful."

"No. No. You're just fine. Please don't cry."

"I need to cry. I need to. I need to." She really did. So she cried for quite a while, and then dropped back to sleep.

The next morning, as we walked down the hall to her room, I could see through the open door and her bed was smooth, freshly made, empty. A new patient had been moved into the other bed in the room, a very old woman whose skeletal hands plucked at a harness that held her down. I kept walking, but it was like moving underwater, and suddenly it was hard to breathe. Then, in the same instant, I heard Nellie's voice and saw her, sitting up in a chair on the far side of her bed. "You'ns come on in here. I'm a-havin' breakfast." She waved her spoon feebly. "Why, I woke up just starved."

The shock was great for all of us. Doctor Fine, a little embarrassed, spoke later that day of a "dramatic temporary recovery." He cautioned us against false hope, and of course he was ultimately right. She only had another twenty days.

After a bowl of Cream O' Wheat, Nellie pawed clumsily at her bed jacket and produced a pack of Winstons. She got one out and I lit it for her.

"I'm a-waitin' *patiently* for that marijuana cigarette, Edwin."

"Yeah, auntie. I'm sorry I . . ."

"Doctor says I can have anything I want. Martinis, by God, if I want 'em."

We all talked for a time, jabbering in our excitement and relief. Then a nurse and a statuesque honey blond in short skirt and high heels came in. They went to the old woman in the bed next to Nellie's.

"Mrs. Schultz, this is the speech therapist, Miss Fuller. She's going to help you learn how to talk again. Isn't that nice?"

Mrs. Schultz made some unintelligible noises, and went back to trying to escape from her harness contraption.

"Mrs. Schultz? I am Miss Fuller. How are you today? Would you like to play a game with me? This game is a voice game." Miss Fuller leaned over the bed and intercepted Mrs. Schultz's hand on its way to the next buckle. "Sometimes we know the words but we forget how to say them, don't we? Now listen to me, Mrs. Schultz. A-a-a-a. Say A-a-a-a."

Mrs. Schultz gurgled.

"*Very* good, Mrs. Schultz. You like this game, don't you? Now as I say a-a-ah, you put your fingers here." Miss Fuller pressed the bony hand to her own warm, full throat. "A-a-a-a. A-a-a-a."

Mrs. Schultz gargled.

"*Very, very* good, Mrs. Schultz. You're doing just *wonderfully.*" As Mrs. Schultz loosened her belts and flaps, the nurse cinched them back up again. "Now let's try a whole word. Do you like apples, Mrs. Schultz? I'll bet you do. Now say a-a-apple. A-a-a-pple." The gags and grunts gradually began to reveal a resemblance, if not to "apple," then to one another. Satisfied, Miss Fuller removed the old woman's hand from her throat and strode out.

There was a brief silence.

"Hey, I wanted to try that," I said, gazing after the therapist's snapping heels. "Let me put my fingers on there and see if I can't say apples."

Jess crowed, the white spikes of his moustache pointing skyward. Ollie Mae hid behind her hand.

"I'd choke 'er," Nellie said, and stuck out the little mushroom of her tongue.

THE LEGEND OF GREAT UNCLE JIM AND THE WOMAN BEHIND IT ALL

The lady in rhinestone glasses at the Winner's Inn wasn't just sure how you got to Tuscarora. She knew it was eighty miles from downtown Winnemucca, and believed there was pavement as far as Golconda, but after that it was all back roads, and likely no signs. I should ask at the hardware store, where they had county maps.

The hardware lady—clean levis, hair dyed jet black, an evergreen smell—helped me to find the right map. Elko County is about the size of Delaware, and appears to be mostly back roads. The roads run in long and lonesome lines through immense sagebrush basins bounded by worn but impressive mountains.

The region is inhabited mainly by jackrabbits and jet fighters, with an occasional faroff peg of a man aboard a horse. Sometimes in the basins there is a slate-green river (forks of the Owyhee or Humboldt); sometimes a wide, shallow lake; sometimes a mirage. Ranches hereabouts run from little ones of five thousand acres to good-sized spreads of a hundred thousand acres or more. From a rise in the road you occasionally see one: a distant clump of poplars, not bright green but at least different, maybe a glitter of aluminum from a trailer. What you will see mostly is rabbits.

Mines came before the ranches. All over the map you can see the little crossed picks and shovels: Old Timer's, Silver Cloud, Midas, Little Jewel. Tuscarora was the biggest in the whole northeast corner of the state until

1904, when the price of silver and the depth of the shafts didn't figure out right and they began to pull the pumps and let the water take over. At one time the population was given as ten thousand—probably on the high side the way all miner's estimates are—but it was mostly tents, a little wood and less brick. Now the hardware lady guessed twenty people might be living there, but no motel, no store, not even a bar, and the road was one of those checkered lines identified as a "gravel road, not graded or drained." Might be tricky this season, she said. They'd been seeing some rain up there. A Volvo? Maybe. She looked vaguely encouraging.

The mountains were shrouded in high mist and light squalls were blowing through when I took the Golconda exit. Gray rain. And raining also in my heart—to embroider a little C & W on the edge of this tale—since I left Reno, where the dark-eyed waitress at Harrah's said it was a good pass and she would have been more than happy to consider it but she had plans after work to catch the tail end of Charlie Daniels' last set, and next week when Willie Nelson went through it was the day before her birthday and she had a date with her dad. I wondered if I was still younger than her dad and told her again about her smile and ordered another whisky, because there was some chance, maybe a good chance, she was lying.

I hadn't planned this essay in historical research very carefully. It was just a loose chip from my childhood, an Ancient Mariner charm or virus that I picked up, listening by the woodbox while my dad and my uncle Jess told the story of Great Uncle Jim, the family's only honest-to-God straight-up-and-down hero. Of course they also told bear stories, and tried to figure out how the Bakers were related to Quannah Parker's Comanches, and retold their own father's exploits as a cowpuncher on the Chisolm trail. But the saga of Uncle Jim in Tuscarora was the big story, I could see that. They told it more often and they told it differently. Still in his galluses and ironpants from a day in the woods, my father would lean forward and grip his knees in his big-knuckled hands and shout at my uncle.

"A big man by God."

"Mountain of a man." Jess always spoke as if Dad had gotten it wrong.

"He did for that sonofabitch."

Jess would snort and look away into the ceiling. "Did for him? Jesus Christ, did for him? Cut his goddamned head off, is what he did."

And so they would go back and argue over the whole thing again. How Jim had been carving on the hitching post with the clasp knife, how the other had approached, what they had most likely said, whether the other man had shot Jim in the alley or in the basement under the saloon, and on and on.

I knew other stories like that. In fact once Dad had come in from fighting fire to tell my awestruck mother that a trail boss, one of the Reed boys, had shot one of the loggers who got drunk and came for him with an axe. That didn't kill him though, Dad observed in some disgust, it was the other dumb drunk sonsofbitches who tried to pack him out and didn't know how.

But Great Uncle Jim was different because he was our own blood. He wasn't in any picture books, or famous anywhere else, but he was all ours. My grandfather had known him personally. He was a big man, a mountain of a man, strong as a bull, and he died full of lead with his boots on. At that age I read a lot of Zane Grey and trashier stuff as well, and it was easy for me to elaborate on the skeletal ballad my dad and uncle were chanting. I could see Big Jim in my mind's eye, see the street, the dustdevils and tumbleweed, the weatherbeaten buildings, the horses shying and stomping in apprehension.

Some of the details made me uncomfortable, and to myself I fudged around them to get the heroic action I needed. It seemed to me Uncle Jim should have a gun too, a blazing gun, and he should walk up the middle of mainstreet toward the other, saying finally, "All right you dirty sidewinding _____, go for your iron!" or the like. But it wasn't like that, I really knew. It was surely much more like the *Lovelock Tribune* had it in their edition of June 6, 1909:

SHOT THROUGH THE HEAD

HE MUSTERED SUFFICIENT STRENGTH TO SEVER

HIS OPPONENT'S HEAD WITH A KNIFE

In one of the bloodiest battles ever recorded in the annals of the state, James Baker and Clyde Thompson, two residents of Tuscarora, fought to their death Sunday night about 8 o'clock.

There were no witnesses to the awful affray—the men fighting their battle alone. After the fight, Baker alone remained alive, and from him the meager particulars obtainable were received.

The two men met on the street and angry words passed between them. Challenges were issued and accepted and the men went into an alley away from the gaze of chance passers-by, to settle their grievances. Very soon four shots, fired from a pistol in the hands of Thompson rang out, and Baker fell to the ground badly wounded, one of the shots taking effect in the head and two in the abdomen. Although wounded unto death, Baker managed to arise and grappled his assailant. The men wrestled and fought until Thompson fell to the ground with Baker on top. Baker then managed to take from his pocket an ordinary pocket knife and with this weapon he inflicted frightful injuries upon Thompson. In an awful frenzy, maddened by the fearful pain he was suffering, and with his strength fast ebbing away, Baker held Thompson while he wielded his knife across his throat. When Baker had finished his butchery, Thompson was practically dead with his throat cut from ear to ear. A later inspection of the remains of Thompson, who died immediately after receiving the wounds, revealed a ghastly spectacle. It was found that the head was almost entirely severed from the body.

Baker and Thompson came from Texas a couple of years ago and had been living in Tuscarora and in that vicinity ever since. Baker was a married man and at the time of the affray his wife was visiting in Elko.

Both men were well known by a number of people in Lovelock. Baker has been in and out of here for the past year. He was a large, raw-boned man and had a glass eye, and was built on the Buffalo Bill order.

I was on the gravel road not graded or drained now, climbing gradually. The plain fell away in a long sweep to the south, in colors of ash, rust, and ghost green. To the north and east the mountains reared, pocked and rotten rock breaking through the flanks of some, a light shawl of snow on the highest. Between these peaks and the thunderheads stacked above them were caverns of shadow, gunmetal blue and dark gray with sometimes a tone of rare, deep mauve.

For twenty minutes I didn't pass a vehicle, and then a muddy old Chevy ton-and-a-half truck with no fenders and a load of hay went by. The two inside looked at me flat from under their wide brims and didn't smile. The ruts had set like ridges of concrete and the Volvo slathered along in them, the steering wheel jumping under my hands with its own life.

Lonesome country. That brings up another bothersome detail of the Uncle Jim story, a detail that as a boy I had little use for, but which now, especially now, suggests itself as perhaps the central one, and maybe explains why I was driving myself ruthlessly over this God-forsaken eighty miles. Dad and Uncle Jess used to refer in a veiled way to "that woman." The Woman Behind It All. When I was eight I didn't know what it was women were behind, and certainly didn't think one of them without even being present could push those two men into the alley and lay them out there in each other's blood. But now I know. Just now I was in fact myself remembering and trying hard not to remember a sweet smile, a beautiful behind, a cheating heart—a combination that can cause one considerable grief. I was right in that time when everything you ever said or did to her appears wrong, when she seems more powerful and glorious and radiant, in your overheated memory, than the mere human you took for a movie and pizza; the time also when this vision suddenly chills and darkens because a shadow has crept beside it, a faceless shadow that she turns to, smiles at, reaches for, kisses, tongues, opens. . . .

A shock as from crossed wires and a burned smell. For your own welfare, from a sense that you are teasing something that is too mad and ravenous for the cages of your mind, you jerk away. There is a numb time. The fenceposts flicker past. Then a word from an old song or a scene from happier times starts the deadly loop all over again.

I smoked for a few miles, because that is one of the things I do at these times. Besides propositioning cocktail waitresses and Keno girls. Maybe because they wear black. Then I pulled up at a place, a scatter of shacks and corroded trailers trying to squeeze under half a dozen ragged cottonwoods. Kirby's Midas Tavern said OPEN but wasn't. Parked in yards were various vehicles, mostly not operable, but one trailer had a wash flapping out back in the cold wind. I got to the front door and there was a phlegmatic man in a plaid shirt to meet me. Yep it was the right road to Tuscarora back there at the fork over the bridge. Might or might not be passable. He had seen a little foreign job go over it yesterday, so maybe. Nothing there, in the way of accommodations. He stopped, blank, so I turned and left.

Maybe the old woman was dead anyway. Distant Cousin Earl, an affable teacher of industrial arts from Sacramento, one summer four years ago drove his spanking RV to Tuscarora to investigate the family legend. He reported that he met an octogenerian lady who had lived in the town all her life, and who as a girl of nineteen had listened to the excited gossip at the stage depot on that June afternoon when two men died. So there was some-body who might know things about this last detail, this Woman Behind It All.

But only gossip. Dinnertime gossip seventy years old. It was beginning to look less and less like a sensible day. Maybe I didn't care whether the old lady was still alive, or whether she could remember anything if she was, or whether what she could remember would reveal anything to me. Maybe I was just driving, and driving now in steeper country, swatches of dirty snow along the roadside, so I could think about how her hair cascaded down over that beautiful behind and how she came to me sometimes like a wave from the other side of the ocean, and think safely about such things, not being able to put my head in my hands and bawl, because my hands had to be on the wheel, still spinning and jerking from the hard ruts.

It is another thing you can do, besides smoke and make hopeless passes. You can drive. I had done it before. The first time especially. If you've heard this one don't stop me.

A man has a job and a house and a car and a wife and a kid. He loves them all and worries about them approximately in that order. For years they hold together; they interlock: the wife takes the kid in the car to the school while the man does his job and then for a few hours they all fall asleep in the house and leave it again early in the morning. One year small things change. A neighbor drives the kid to school but the wife disappears with the car any-way. The man pursues the job so far he does not fall back into the house some evenings. There are parties and dinners and some people leave before others. Finally some people don't even go. Glassware may be broken. Things are said which have a magical effect of suddenly diminishing greatly both the person speaking and the person spoken to. One day the wife takes the kid in the car and does not come back, ever, to fall asleep in the house.

The man gets another car and he drives. He drives perhaps all night. Sometimes he gets someplace, where he smokes a lot, and drinks too, and makes passes at people. Or he drives around looking for her, the WBIA, parks near her house, waits. Perhaps she arrives finally and is with someone else, the shadow, and he can hear them laugh in anticipation on the way to the front door. So he begins driving again.

We must talk about violence now. In my case, not that uncommon, it was the self hurting the self. I cut myself and tried to take too many pills, but not very seriously. Some of my friends did it much better with the bottle and the automobile. An odd thing, that when The Woman goes away or at least plays away, a man looks for a quiet room where he can hack himself or eat oblivion. Not everyone of course. These are modern times. There is a new school of thought, according to which one is cool, one shrugs, one keeps an "open relationship." I have seen a few of these open arrangements up close. One from very close. I want to report that I find, beneath the casual laughter, the worldly winks, the arch jokes, the same hard and horny core of hate, the same murderous undertow that exists in the ghettos of common love.

These days everybody is a shrink, so everybody knows that the modern man who turns the blade on himself or goes in for revenge fucking is only taking a substitute. What he really wants to do is kill the two of them, or at least the rival, but society frowns on this sort of direct action.

The implication is, must be, that to take such steps is a serious aberration, not to be countenanced. A whole rhetoric has grown up to mask these raw animal feelings. I understand your position. My needs are not being met. We have to communicate honestly. I respect you. The children are the most important thing. We have to stay friends. Friends. Thought I'd drop over, friend, and try out this double-barreled twelve gauge.

Perhaps some people do not believe in these powerful and sinister emo-

tions. Perhaps most men are only "upset" or "disappointed." Perhaps only a few discover such Neanderthal strata in themselves. But when I watch my friends go down into divorce, I see the same external signs I know so well. The nicotine insomnia, the sudden and indiscriminate lust, a pale and haggard mien that reminds one of consumption, an inner, eating fire. They've got the tiger by the tail.

So maybe I am a rare and dangerous Neanderthal aberrant, and so was Uncle Jim. Western genes. I do know that the second time around it got just as rough. A very modern affair, this second one. Massage and good dope and the Sierras. A blonde. She ran into a Jewish psychiatrist with a swimming pool in Marin. And I began to understand some things. I understood the Nazis. I even understood David Berkowitz, the chubby young man who could not resist the thrill of firing a .44 magnum point-blank into the faces of pretty girls. I understood rape. On certain days directly after sensing the first nub of my antlers I saw some very terrible little movies inside my skull, while I drove the Volvo around like a zombie. The psychiatrist did not get off easily either.

I was not proud of being the producer of these ghastly little flicks. But they were hard to control. I thought I might be crazy and sought help. Of course it had to be another Jewish psychiatrist. With detachment he helped me to translate the horror shows scene by scene into the new rhetoric. He encouraged me to talk this language to others, and indeed after a time I did not feel so weird and began to think nice thoughts about my ex. You know, communication and acceptance. Two years later we all three chatted around the swimming pool and admired their new baby. We were modern and normal again.

The rain picks up and the mud ridges are now slick on the surface. It occurs to me that I could be stranded here all night if I try to straighten out one of these curves. Since the haytruck I have encountered only two four-wheel-drive pickups, traveling fast, the drivers at the last moment lifting two fingers from the steering wheel in an ambiguous gesture. I have a bag of oranges from my tree in California and one thin Mexican blanket, which is not much to pit against a gusty and moonless night on this high desert. But after making a couple of hills in second gear I drop into another of the basins and see on the other side a cluster of buildings perched on the side of a considerable peak. Mount Blitzen, according to the map.

On the last rise before town I see higher on the mountain some tailing heaps and a ruined smelter chimney. Otherwise Tuscarora is mostly weathered trailers, a few sagging frame houses, and one geodesic dome covered in asphalt paper. All of them try to squeeze under a dozen ragged cottonwoods. Beside the post office there is one square, ancient adobe building, but the windows are boarded shut. I park in what looks like the middle of whatever this is, and see a wooden sign MUSEUM on the back porch of one old house. A woman in a down jacket, supported by a cane, moves toward me from another house across the street and we exchange pleasantries. No she is not the particular old woman I am looking for. I must be after either Dela Phillips here at the museum or Nona Trembath in the white house at the end of the street there. They're both over eighty. Both been here always. Ring long and hard at Dela's. Hard of hearing.

I thank her and walk up the steps to begin ringing long and hard. Dela may be hard of hearing, but she certainly does not look eighty. Hair dyed a bright carrot, she still fills her loose rayon blouse and her eyes are huge and warm behind coke bottle lenses. I introduce myself as I am led into the museum, also her living room, and she brightens.

"Why sure they was two of them and one had a wife, her name was Edna, and a kid too I think. And man number two come along and they was something went on before, used to be his wife then I think, and they fought out there in the street. There was a saloon right across from that old brick building and they rolled down in the cellar under it. One had a gun and the other a knife I think but I don't know who shot who. Which one was your uncle?"

"The one with the knife."

"That was one of them, all right. I was only eleven, you know. We had the dinner station where the stage came in, and I heard the people talk about it. We fed seventy-five people a day there sometimes."

The porch windows are stacked full of old pink and violet tonic bottles, lending an Edgar Allan Poe hint to the light. In the main room there are glass cases full of chunks of rock frosted with crystals, cut stones and turquoise, and an assortment of combs, carbide headlamps, button hooks, revolvers, cuff links, crimpers, augurs, and the like. On the wall, several racks from big bull elk; also a row of guns including a Sharps buffalo rifle and several Winchester and Henry repeaters. Also many pictures of men beside steam engines or on ore cars: burly, moustachioed men not given to hilarity. Other pictures of twelve-horse wagons stacked with sagebrush (Dela explains that the smelter ate up all the brush for miles around; five hundred chinamen grubbed it out with hoes). The usual heyday hilltop views of a sprawl of tents divided by roads of churned mud.

"So everybody was scared to go down there, wouldn't even get close to the saloon. Finally they heard one man hollering and they came to see. I don't know which one it was—"

"My uncle."

"—one of them hollered out 'Come and git me I don't want to die here with this sonofabitch.' They pulled him out but the other was already dead, cut up something awful. The other didn't live too long after that. Your uncle. Where was he from?"

"Texas, I think."

"That probably accounts for some of it." Dela laughs. "They say." She moves to one wall beside an old pedal pump organ. "Here's a picture of that woman. Edna."

It was one of those man and wife portraits in a little oval frame with a cloudy backdrop, woman in the foreground and turned a little to one side, below her master. Hard to tell about these images of femininity from bygone times; the coiffures and starch and whalebone usually obscure whatever it is that made the blood leap then. But this time I think I can see it. A petite woman, dark eyes and hair, though perhaps a little full in the cheeks for the small, fine nose. Not exactly a smile, but just conceivably that other expression that goes a shade beyond a smile in the direction of the devil's casino.

"That fella ain't either one of them. He was my husband's uncle. She married him afterward and they moved East. So she got into the Phillips, my family."

Dela beams at me, happy at this relation, however distant. Then there is a tremendous shock of thunder and the pink bottles chatter excitedly on the sills.

"Sonic boom." Dela nods reassuringly at me, and waves generally west. "It's the Navy over there."

The Navy, of course.

"We had a big ranch. Not big like Spanish ranch, but we had ten thousand deeded acres and three thousand head of cattle. We sold out to Bing Crosby." She pauses and I murmur. "Yes, we knew him and his family real well. They come here often but then of course they sold it after he died. Here I'll show you the gun that killed the first man in Tuscarora."

I look at the old Colt under the glass. "Interesting," I say and tap the case. "Were there lots of murders here?"

Dela laughs. "Oh no. Tuscarora wasn't a real wild town. One man shot over a water deal I remember. Oh of course when the range hands got through with riding for two months and got their three days they would hit for town on horseback and when they got to the top of the hill they'd start shooting and come at a dead run. After three days in town they'd have to go back and the boss would come around to the saloons then and settle up for their damage. You know just busted glass and chairs and such."

I pause before a magnificent slab of polished, petrified wood.

"Sequoias." Dela shakes her head. "Thousands of years ago you know those sequoias, that's the big redwoods, went from coast to coast. This whole country was tropical then you know."

I examine the red and yellow whorls of the grain.

"Were the mines going then, in 1909?"

"They was downhill then. Last big mine closed in 1916. Hardly anything left of those days now. That big adobe block building there. Used to be the lodge building, Masonic and Odd Fellows and Knights of Pythias all together. Would you sign the register?"

71

I notice behind the register a hand-lettered sign that lists the admission at one dollar. I pull out two.

"I'm paying double, ma'am, for all your help. And I want to take some pictures. Now what happened to all that machinery?"

"Why thank you sir. There was all kinds of machinery for a while, all those pumps and engines and the little ore cars you know just rusting away. Between wars they picked it all up and sent it to Japan. For scrap."

Japan, of course.

I shoot a few pictures, thank Edna for her time, and then ask about Nona Trembath.

"White house on the corner. Now she'll tell you all about that business. She's older than I am you know." She blinks the huge brown eyes and smiles. "Sure enjoyed it."

Walking down the muddy street under a cavernous sky, the cloud cover now showing a rift or two as the wind stiffens, I think about those men in armbands and narrow collars and moustaches. How they handled the open relationship. I know I wouldn't care to be a party in any such arrangement with most of them. I suppose they came to this place, these vistas of empty air and dry plain and ugly rock, for the silver and gold, which meant for the money and the power, the silk and the wine and the cheroots, which meant ultimately the women. And most of them didn't find it. But that didn't get rid of the need. The Big Need. Men's needs were probably not being met here in Tuscarora in 1909.

A little bell tinkles when you open Nona's gate, just for the opener's pleasure. For Nona there is a regular doorbell. I see her coming through the window in the door, warped a little in the glass. She looks under five feet, but erect in a faded cotton dress. She too wears thick spectacles, and over the right lens is taped a square blue wrapper from some powder or tablet. I am directly invited into the cluttered, too-warm room, and state my business.

She commands me to sit in the overstuffed chair and then she begins at the beginning and lets me have the whole thing, pausing just a moment for me to finish fumbling with my notepad, speaking in bright, flat prose.

"Yes, Baker and Thompson. One was one-eyed, a great big nigger. Baker I think that was. Happened on Celebration Day. Thompson was stayin' here in town. Real quiet fella. Never said nothin' to nobody. Baker was working on a ranch, Roseberry's place. He was a real bulldog. They say he'd slip off a wagon and throw a steer right flat on the ground. Had a wife or said it was his wife that he kept on the ranch there. Anyway after this Thompson came around he spied on 'em I guess and this particular day he and Baker started something and then walked down the alley by the saloon. The real fight started there. People heard shooting. I guess they rolled down into the cellar and for a long time everybody was afraid to come near, but finally this Baker threw the cellar doors back and walked out. He said 'I won't die in there with that sonofabitch. I did for him though.' But he never lived past seven o'clock that night. The other fella had his head cut almost off, just a little skin holding it. I know that because my dad helped the doctor sew it back on. People asked Baker what the trouble was and he said 'Ask Shorty.' But when the sheriff went to find Shorty he had cleared out. To Idaho. The other thing this Baker said before he died was 'Do something for me. Don't bury me in the same grave with that sonofabitch.' But they did anyway. This is hard ground. Well everybody figured that woman was Thompson's wife somewhere else and this Baker run off with her, and come here and introduced her as his own. But the funny thing was a few months later the sheriff got a letter from a woman out in Nebraska or someplace asking about this Jim because she said she was his wife and wanted to know if there was anything left, like an estate. There wasn't anything of course but an old saddle and bridle not worth much."

Somewhere in this tight weave I got in a question about the one eye, and Nona said yes she was sure about that. He was a good fella too, cordial, and could pitch hay like the dickens. Then the postmistress tapped and came in, and they talked about an unfortunate accident two nights ago. An old man died in a headon collision on Highway 95 out of Winnemucca. "He was eighty

73

years old and wouldn't wear glasses, that's why," Nona observed. They moved on to talk about the square dance coming up. The postmistress said they might even have enough for two squares.

During this interlude I am still thinking of the woman in Nebraska who wasn't the WBIA but who was the other kind, the Woman Left Out. Probably left on a bleak sodhut homestead with a band of ragged, whining children. Left for a little tramp with something deadly in her near-smile. Why does a WLO stick it through, raise the kids, plant and plow, bake bread and gather cow chips, while the man with his Big Need turns to murder? I am speaking of a general pattern, knowing of many exceptions, those Frankies who toted forty-fours into barrooms or took their men apart with a razor. But generally not. Generally men do it.

I do know the feeling, if not the reasons. There is some connection with the children. In our time women take the kids when they leave, and whether fair or not it releases some deep, dangerous force in a man. After the first numb horror you go molten at the core, something rears and begins to rage. Every nerve twangs to some ancient battle song. When it happened to me, that first time, I felt the voltage in my nervous system take a quantum leap. I slept maybe four hours a night for a month, smoked three packs of cigarettes a day, and scrawled pages full of drivel. I also hatched plots. Shoot him with my deer rifle, take my daughter and hijack a plane to Cuba. Attuned to such possibilities, I began to notice how much of that was going on in the daily newspapers. In the very city I was living in somebody tried it; he holed up in a maintenance shed at the airport with his child and made demands, mostly on his ex-wife. The FBI sharpshooters did for him and his Neanderthal genes. The kid was unharmed, though spattered with her daddy's blood.

Most of the time I knew in some chamber of the brain that these fantasies would not be realized, were only some kind of imperfect psychic pressure valve. Outwardly I taught classes and went to committee meetings and mowed the lawn, and smiled and thanked the neighbors who brought sympathetic hot dishes to the Abandoned One. But the heaving magma was still there inside. A wise old friend came to visit and told me I was still normal. However, the tremendous energy I felt was an illusion. "You probably think you can uproot trees," he said. "Actually you are very tired and probably not functioning at peak efficiency." Maybe so, but during that month I built a hell of a fence, played some outstanding touch football, and wrote the only sonnets of my career. And no experience of my lifetime has ever matched this one, the loss of wife and child, for sheer savage intensity. I felt positively luminous with adrenalin, and if ever I was capable of—or thought with relish about—walking down a dusty alley to meet another man with a gun, it was then.

After the postmistress leaves we shift the conversation to Nona herself. She has removed the paper wrapper patch from her spectacles, and her eyes are magnified like Dela's, but they are a different, odd color. It is the color of this country, a subtle blend of gray and green and brown.

"I'll be ninety come the 13th of October. I was married a year or two after we're talkin' about, 1911, to a Welshman. We saved up and bought a ranch to get him out of the mines. He was a Cousin Jack, we called 'em. Welshmen and Cornishmen. Good miners. In one of the other big mines they had Irish, so the shifts had to quit at different hours, otherwise the Jacks and the Irish fought all the time. We bought 878 acres and a hundred head of cows and ran it until he died in 1941. Bad lungs, from the mines. Nicest man you'd ever want to know."

One of the lucky ones, I think. There were three men for every woman in this territory then. And Nona is pretty clearly not an ordinary woman.

"First thing I had to do after he died was prove up title. My name wasn't on anything, just his. I spent three thousand dollars on lawyers and accountants and assessors to keep that place. And I ran it myself. When I sold it in the fifties—you know who I sold it to?"

I shake my head but I think I already know.

"Bing Crosby. Yes sir. And when I sold it I had 1700 acres, 200 head of sheep, 250 head of cows and I put up 250 measured tons of hay every damn year. I wasn't sittin' down."

I keep a respectful silence.

"I wrote a story about that and they printed it in the Elko paper, I'll show you. And the *Deseret News* in Salt Lake sent a man here and they wrote me up."

She is swift on her feet and knows just where the clippings are. I look them over. Woman Runs Ranch by Herself. Gal with Gumption. Pictures of Nona in overalls and short hair beside her saddled horse. Her life laid out in the same level talk over sixty-eight column inches, including two paragraphs on Great Uncle Jim.

"I got five proposals of marriage after that *Deseret News* story. Men just wrote from anywhere, even Canada." She laughs. "One fella wanted to know just how many head of cows I was running, before he completed his proposal."

She was, I suggest, interested? Oh no. One man and he was the nicest you could want.

What is it women want out of men?

"Kindness." Quick as a rattler. "See her wants before she does."

I work on that by myself for a while.

"Say, you want to see an ounce of gold?"

She returns from a back room with a little clear plastic locket full of dull yellow grains.

"Got that chain from Buckskin Jack. He wanted to know where the gold came from." She sees me smiling.

"Oh I know some fellas with nicknames." She looks at me sideways, devilish. "Buckskin Jack he was a big nigger like you."

"You got a name for me?"

"Don't know you well enough yet."

"I'll bet you make up those names."

"I do no such thing now. You just look, I got a list of 'em and everybody is somebody I knew or heard about. Look here."

She produces a sheet of paper from her album and I read through the collection:

Flyspeck Bill, Crooked Neck McCray, Dirty Shirt George, Cream Puff Ike, 25 Pinky, The Denver Sheik, Fade Away Kid, Chippie Chaser, Tamale, Silk Hat Harry, Bolts and Nuts, Seldom Seen Slim, Snake River Pete, Gimme Kid, Scissor Beak, and of course Buckskin Jack.

Then there is Gold Tooth Bess, Broken Nose Helen, Dirty Neck Grace, and Bull Shit Alice.

"Some women here too."

"The Sportin' Girls. There was a big Sportin' House here. These people come from all over—the Klondike, Australia, Wales."

"Couldn't hide their flaws."

"Land no, everybody got a name right away."

"Were there fights over these sporting ladies?"

"No, not much. Fellas didn't seem to fight over them."

A pause, while I work to come to the question I realize I have been heading for, have driven six hundred miles to ask.

"Why do men do that?"

"What: sportin'?"

"No. I mean why do they kill each other, like Baker and Thompson?"

"That's nature. You see a lot of that."

She waits, alert and confident, but no followup question occurs to me.

"Not so much like that nowadays. Now there's always something else comin' along."

I keep silent, wondering if that makes the difference. What if I had not been able to foresee another after the first, and again after the second? What if this last one, still haunting the freeway with me, were the absolute last? What if no waitress or Keno girl would ever smile at me again except to increase her tip? Would nature then push me to murder?

It could not be that simple. Mr. Thompson did not have to hunt Edna down; there must have been others available—at least Bull Shit Alices—in Omaha or St. Louis or Abilene. It must have been partly the child. Perhaps men have a horror of their barrenness, a desire to perpetuate and extend their identity, a desire which if frustrated becomes violent. Zoologists tell us

77

that the males of a species often fight to insure that the most aggressive and durable genes will be transmitted to progeny. The female merely waits, provocative, at the edge of the field of battle; she only need exercise her blind urge to turn her tail to the victor. Her place in history is already assured. The male can plant his seed, shape his race after his own image only by conquest, and in most species he is put to the test of battle each season.

Among many ungulates, walrus, and some primates, the defeated males become mournful exiles. Some have grown too old, and in one short, bloody encounter have lost whole harems. Once whipped, the stud cannot approach his former loving mates, who ignore him or even slash at him in contempt. Sometimes they do not live long after their loss of power; sometimes they collect in a spiritless fraternity and graze out their days on poor and stony ground. Give them an intense consciousness of their lot, an ability to conceive their own desolate future, and perhaps you have the formula for mad lust and destruction, herds of Nazi mustangs thundering through the streets of Reno, frothing to violate and kill. But I guess I would have such imaginary Hun-hordes start with the nuclear testing stations, or the Navy over there.

"But it was a better world then than it is now," Nona goes on without me. "These poisons they're putting in the ground. These wastes. Why that stuff just doesn't go away you know. Terrible. But our worst problem is the refugees."

I look inquiring.

"Yes, hell, where are we going to put them? Thousands and thousands coming in now from El Salvador. We haven't got the room. And those Cubans. They were just crooks. What are we going to do with them?"

I don't know.

"People don't know what's going to happen any more. A fella come around here a few years back, wanted to look at a mine I have a little interest in. Wanted a shelter, a storehouse with food and water and guns underground. Big old fat pious nigger he was. Had lots of money. Why I told him he was crazy. What's the point of living if everybody else is gone, I said to him. That's damn fool craziness."

I agree. We talk over a few other world affairs, then get back to her life. I ask if she was ever lonesome during those twenty years spent running cattle on seventeen hundred acres of hard ground.

"Oh no. If you got a ranch you got no time to be lonesome."

It occurs to me all at once that I have not asked about children, but she has seen where I am headed before I do.

"I lost five children, I did. Never had any children." She bites her lip when she smiles this time.

"Your children? You had—"

"I didn't have 'em. I carried 'em. Four, five months usually. Couldn't keep them. Not enough water in my womb, I think. Something." She is biting hard on her lip now, and there is a just perceptible shake in her voice.

I fumble out a story about my grandmother, who had nine, she always said, although two only lived for a few hours. Those two she always counted and you could tell she cared about them. It is neither the right nor the wrong thing to offer. I stare at the clippings to keep from looking at her, and after a while one of us thinks of something to say and we go on.

Another tap at the door, and I let in a little man with straight brown hair, freckles, and buck teeth.

"This is my boyfriend, comes to see me every day almost."

"Hiya Nona," he says and takes a seat. "What's your name?"

"Will."

"Mine's Rick."

"He's lived in every state in the union except Alaska and Hawaii," Nona volunteers.

"My dad's a millwright."

"How old are you?"

"Eight."

"Every state?"

"Except Hawaii and Alaska," Nona reminds me.

"Yeah. We was in Arizona last year. I hope we go back there. Where do you live?"

"California."

He looks noncommital.

I see the landscape darkening outside, and begin my thank-yous, preparing to leave. Then I remember the oranges, and trot out to the Volvo and get half a dozen for her. When she tells me to come back, she means it, though neither of us believes it will happen. I drive away, leaving this ninety-year-old and her boyfriend of eight to their own rare and special romance.

When I pass Midas the western sky is the color of stainless steel and I need headlights. The rabbits are suddenly everywhere. These are big, gray Western Jacks with ears and tails tipped in black. Soon I am swerving, skidding, braking, trying to avoid them. The spears of light make them crazy and stupid; they freeze or run the wrong way. Once I count four at once weaving figure eights in front of me. Inevitably, with a curse, I hit one. Then another.

Dodging this way, I think of the beautiful behind only intermittently, a little wearily. The next-to-last cigarette in the pack tastes dry and bitter, and I am finally feeling the mileage. I am also feeling ashamed. The legend of Great Uncle Jim and the Woman Behind It All. That little bit of a ranch lady back there is worth six of them. She lost five, died inside five times, and was driven to kill nobody, but to run more sheep and more cattle on more land.

Nature, she would say. Maybe that's it. When it comes down to it they are stronger. They don't need us, except for seed, and it drives us crazy. Our nature to be crazy. Or are there three kinds, the WBIA and the WLO and the Woman Above It All. And all three of them drive us crazy, crazy as these rabbits, Jesus hundreds of them, now I have hit four. They take the children or they lose the children, and we go wild. We drive the jets and set off the bombs and grub for the gold and kill each other. Or ourselves.

I hit the fifth rabbit and there is nothing but a little jerk at the corner of my mouth. Because of the sound. The terrible sound.

LETTER TO A NEBRASKA HOUSEWIFE

Dear Lady,

In one of your bad dreams, a motorcycle rackets down the country road, and, before you have time to think, to grab your robe and flick on the bedlamp and call out, the engine coughs and dies; you hear the cicadas stop short and a shadow, darker than the darkness, appears at the open bedroom window and then passes swiftly over the sash, to crouch there in the dim silence with you. A low, harsh breathing.

You suck in air to scream, but even as your throat tightens there is a flash of moonlight along a blade and you find every muscle paralyzed, the air in your lungs suspended. Your eyes suddenly fill with tears and you cannot stifle a tiny, hard sob.

A gust of wind billows the curtains aside bringing moonlight and the sound of sycamore leaves. In the brief wash of light something about his clothing shines, like scales. In silhouette you can see shaggy hair, but the face remains black, black, black. Two tiny stars glitter in the eye caverns, and you know he is looking straight at you. From some unknown, insane pressure, your breathing has fallen into rhythm with his, and you wait, still paralyzed, for his voice. You expect a coarse demand, but what comes is a low, rasping laughter: "I howl my joy."

He is moving now, still laughing, the blade is lifting, and you cave in to your knees, head up and mouth open. And what ensues then: the hot wet blows, the shuddering, the terrible indistinct knowledge, the forcing, widening, rending—all this remains ill-defined. We both know that you would endure unspeakable acts, acts whose mere suggestion provokes a disgust so profound that your mind recoils before an image can form. Yet these unimaginable things happen. They will happen more and more often now. No more "crime in the streets." Instead, crime in your very bedroom, kitchen, and basement (that's where Perry methodically blew out the brains of the Clutter family) and crime of a very personal, physical kind. Yes, good lady, "crime" means all of those unspeakable acts, but especially what your local paper will describe as "cold-blooded murder" and "senseless killing" and "sexual assault."

Yet you have been a kind soul, perhaps devout, certainly a believer in the power of Christian mercy. You may have contributed funds for the Hungarian refugees, for the victims of the Chilean earthquake, for the starving Biafrans and Ethiopians. You surely pass on your outmoded clothes and appliances to the needy crippled and poor of St. Vincent's or Good Will. You save the last piece or two of cake for the smallest child. Your garden furnished zucchini to the whole neighborhood. Believe me, in a thousand ways you command my affection and respect (emotions made keener by a whisper of nostalgia), for the warmth and sustenance you provide so unstintingly are the compost necessary to the flourishing of any hope for the human spirit.

Yet—and I must plead here for your indulgence—I want to speak to you of that prowling shadow, created a few paragraphs back, to menace you. Bear with me now, dear lady? Suspend your anger and disgust a little longer. My aim is only to help you—us—foresee what may soon come, to bring us to an understanding of those dark powers, "violence" and "crime," now unleashed in our land; yea, even in the country of clapboard and corn, and hogs, and screen doors, and deep-dish cobblers, and rope swings from big elms.

To help us understand, we must begin by imagining a time before there was a "Nebraska," a time when there were no freeways or supermarkets or radio stations. Then there was only a great sweep of grass, and of course, the buffalo and antelope, the rabbits and prairie dogs, the coyotes and rattlesnakes. Perhaps you have always thought of this land at this time as "empty" or even "uninhabited." But you really know better, don't you? You had it in school; and even now you must see here and there the little re-membrances: the "Teepee Village" motel, with a drawing of a curvaceous Minne-ha-ha in a leather bikini; the Big Chief burger, the knickknack sou-venirs—toy moccasins and tomahawks for kids.

Can you imagine that time, before the Red Men were part of the history of "Nebraska," before they vanished into books? It isn't long ago, really. A few survivors of Sand Creek and Wounded Knee were around when you were a girl. Nor is it hard to envision, with a little help from Hollywood. You know they rode like the wind—no saddle at all and a mere strip of rawhide for a bridle—sending arrows into a buffalo's hump at full gallop.

With your good, country, common, horse sense you can perceive that these people were proud of themselves, superior beings in their own eyes—like all people. Their ways were the true ways, defined and renewed by chief and medicine man year after year. It seemed to them right and honorable to hunt buffalo and steal horses from each other. What they could see of the earth—those endless, endless plains—seemed their natural home, a free gift of the Great Spirit. Thousands of beasts and birds and plants shared this earth with them, were part of the busy pattern of their lives: flint and feathers from this place, quills from that, fish bones from another, lodge poles from the distant hills, red willow bark for smoking from the marsh, bitumen paint out of dry washes. You might have been surprised, yourself a busy bee with PTA and church bazaar, at how much hard honest industry was needed to belong to this society.

You know, too, how such effort becomes dear: the sweat and rage that go into building a house, or paying off a mortgage, into tomato seedlings, into a son's fifth birthday party, into getting that letter to the editor just right, into painting window trim (all corners and ridges)—all these make your world sweet as life itself. In fact, life is unimaginable without your house and trees, with all their sags and crooks, without the familiar sound of chickens, chil-dren, television, and the old John Deere lugging down on the pull; without the gleaming corridors and floating music and soap smells of the super-market, without friends and enemies and gossip.

You know all this because once in a terrible while the thought occurs: what if they were to take all this from us? Our farms taken over by the state, all of us driven into camps, issued gray uniforms, separated from our families, forced to pledge allegiance to a foreign flag, deprived of Lawrence Welk and Roy Acuff, everything written and uttered in an incomprehensible gabble . . .

Those moments of secret horror prove to you how precious is your world. The world of the Oglala was equally dear to them, you understand that, don't you? But within a few years, for them, the horror came to pass. The white man came, not by night, but shining and clanking in open day. At first they wheedled, but then they reached sufficient numbers and simply took. They scraped away the soil to make wide roads, cut trees to build bridges; then built the iron road and fences and towns. Finally, Omaha and Chicago and San Francisco. They always came thickest, like locusts, where they found the yellow stuff in the ground. How amazed the Red Men were at this! White men would slaughter them and each other for a handful of stone!

It did not take long—about forty years—to kill most of the plains Indians and put the rest in concentration camps. They were killed thoroughly, dear lady, men, women, and children alike. Can you imagine that? The charge of tall, fair-skinned men with hair on their faces? Cannon whose thunder would tear off a leg or arm or head? Men all dressed alike who moved in a line and, upon order, cut and chopped at every living thing, like a row of macabre dancers, mocking harvest ceremony? And after all that, the bleak gritty camps in alien territory, where there was always too little to eat, too little to wear, and no hope. Some, of course, tried to escape. They starved or froze or were exterminated as at Bear Paws and Wounded Knee.

The strange, mad cruelty of these assaults must have baffled the Indians, especially when they were preceded by a plea for the new God—gentle, passive Christ who allowed himself to be nailed to a tree without a word of protest. But soon, like black men before them, the Red Men embraced that God, and all the other ways of white men. They had no weapons; their horses were gone; their children forgot the mother tongue; their women were white men's whores. They could die, empty, or try to become like the terrible race who would otherwise exterminate them.

Or . . . they could vanish into myth, becoming a pop symbol for future avengers. A symbol of everything wild and blood-crazed. "Savages." Hollywood created the type—a blood-curdling shriek clothed in paint and feathers. Though of course the cavalry always won (by daylight again, sabers flashing and flags snapping in the wind), the real power of these films could be traced to the fascinating horror of Indian tactics: they crept in the dark forest with arrow and knife, or they swooped down in a surprise attack (Tarnation! Terrorists!). To hone this horror to its finest, excruciating edge, Hollywood had its feathered scowls and shrieks abduct a white woman, rending her modest mother hubbard in the struggle. How our little hearts pumped with anxious terror then, children huddled in the flickering twilight of the front rows, sprinkled with the dirty hail of popcorn and candy wrappers, stinking of kiddy pee! We saw those giant white shoulders loom over us, streaked with a rivulet of bright blood! Our own mothers and first grade teachers stripped and lashed before our starting eyes!

Those terrible images sank into your mind, perhaps, as they did into mine, and are the stuff of which these bad dreams are made. But there is more at stake here: the nightmare trespasses into life. Dark tides of long-maned men surge at the borders of "Nebraska" and in their hearts simmers the rage to murder. (I am frightened too, good lady, but let us try to master the panic and understand.)

Consider: why should we perpetuate this myth of the sneaking savage? The worst carnage was the work of our ancestors—your grandfather and mine. Yellow Wolf tells us how Colonel Gibbon surprised Joseph's people at dawn on the Big Hole, directing cross-fire into their lodges. One bullet, he remembers, tore off the hand of a month-old baby. This, mysteriously, more than the outright slaughter of many other women and children, enraged the braves. James Mooney, an "ethnologist," describes with reluctant certitude how the Seventh Cavalry rode down the fleeing women and children at Wounded Knee and shot them in the snow like so many rabbits. He also tells

of a three-month-old baby girl, dug out of a drift only "slightly frozen" three days after the massacre: she wore a little cap of buckskin upon which was embroidered, in beadwork, an American flag. Touched, the wife of General Colby (commander of the Nebraska troops), adopted her. Or read Mrs. Kroeber's account of the joyous abandon with which degenerate offspring of the forty-niners massacred the Mill Creek Indians—except for Ishi, who finally threw himself on white men's mercy, lived dutifully according to their ways, became momentarily famous as an exhibit in their museum, and then died of their diseases.

But this is all "history," you may say. Over and done with. Unfortunate— tragic even—but beyond redemption. True enough. Redemption is indeed impossible, and this implies that our guilt is ineradicable. The knowledge of these crimes and that other, the long shadow of slavery, haunts us. Red and black. Night and blood. Nigger commies. Dirty devil-spawn hippies. We fear them, because now we know how dear to man is the simple, established order of his life, and hence we infer how much hatred we must bear for having annihilated that order for others.

Ancestral crime (the Bible and Doctor Freud agree) does not wither in time. The Lakotah blood beneath your feet still cries out. Not for revenge— please understand, revenge is not relevant. No, the cry is to the lost and broken still among us, the survivors, and it tells of the bloody horror hidden in the heart of white men. They react, as you yourself react, with hatred born of fear, but their fear is confirmed and energized by their own continuing destruction.

Ours is "projected" as celluloid red devils who are made to perform our atrocities so that we are not forced to hate ourselves. The hardest thing to grasp, dear lady, is that our deepest fears, our nightmares, are rooted in our fearsome selves. All our crimes, from Wounded Knee to My Lai, ride with that angel of death on his roaring motorcycle. In this dream country, we must learn that those who come to destroy, have been destroyed.

Perry Smith, who giggled after he had blown the Clutter family all over their own basement walls, was a half-breed Cherokee. When he wet the bed at night in the orphanage, the hooded nuns beat him with a flashlight.

FATHER WHITE MOUSE

The Americans who still hunt wild game for daily food live in two very different regions. One group, the northerners, inhabits ice-bound coasts and survives mostly on fish, blubber and reindeer. The other group roams tropical and semitropical forestland, where they take a great variety of game, including birds, reptiles, insects, worms, snails, and rodents.

Both these groups are of Asiatic origin, and are presumed to be related. Their common ancestors, we are told, took advantage of low water during a glacial period and hiked across the neck of land connecting Siberia and Alaska. In the next ten thousand years or so these adventurers crossed two continents, learning their way through quite a range of environments: arctic wasteland, tundra, rain forest, alpine slope, grasslands, desert, tropical jungle, bog, and delta. In the course of this journey they killed animals of all sizes, from the mastodon to the mouse, using spears, clubs, darts, snares, hooks, deadfalls, nets, springes, and finally the bow and arrow. Although they ate these creatures regularly and used their hides and bones for shelter and tools, they treated their prey with respect, sometimes with reverence. They told stories featuring animals or their spirits and usually they held such tales to be true, or even sacred.

The hunting story is therefore a very old, respectable way of communicating important knowledge, and I approach it with trepidation. But since, as everyone knows, both these groups of hunters are shrinking away rapidly and since, therefore, the opportunity to tell true stories about them is also vanishing, I must risk this imperfect and amateur account. It is the true story of how my son the monkey was killed by an Asháninka hunter and mourned by choruses of Old MacDonald's Farm.

In the beginning—as the Asháninka say—I knew nothing about the forest. Or only a very little. I knew that in some regions the rivers are huge and the people go about in canoes with outboard motors, while in others there are high mountains shrouded in fog and here everyone walks, except the white newcomers. These newcomers come in single-engined planes on days when the clouds drift apart.

The Asháninka survive in these mist-haunted forests and also along certain rivers that unravel from the white cape of the Peruvian Andes. They are Arawak speakers, linked to the Caribbean and Central America by dugout canoe, and to the whole Amazon basin by their reliance on manioc for strong drink, cotton for their sacklike cushma gown, and palm fronds for the roof over their heads. They do not know how long they have been in these hills, or where they came from, and they do not appear much bothered by their ignorance.

In small thatch huts on the slopes above river courses, they live a very simple life, a kind of life that is probably not very different from that of the forerunners who first drifted into the country on that long trek from the northern snowfields. The women grow the cotton for the cushma and dye, spin and weave it themselves. They also dig, peel, steam, and masticate the yucca root (manioc) which they then spit into a wooden trough of water. Overnight bacteria in the saliva ferment this mixture into *masato*, a strong beer everyone drinks every day.

The men make bows of palm heartwood, and arrows from cane, tree resin, fire-hardened spikes, and feathers. They also clear land with axe and machete, burn the slash, and plant yucca, corn, coffee, tobacco, cocoa, banana, and papaya. While these things are growing, they go hunting for deer, pig, tapir.

Usually they begin these tasks at dawn and work at them until the sun reaches the place we call one o'clock. Then they go home to the masato trough and refresh themselves and talk and sing and laugh until dark. In the childish and backward view of the Asháninka, that is apparently what makes life worthwhile. Only a few of the young, mostly the men, have acquired

higher ambitions. They disappear for months and come back wearing sunglasses, polyester pants, wristwatches, and an uneasy expression.

One day the clouds parted and a plane jounced down on the little grass runway. There was only one passenger. This was Big White Mouse, the foolish romantic. He had always been big, shy, and myopic, but he actually got his name only a decade ago, during the brief war at Wounded Knee, South Dakota. There he discovered that he did not have the courage to fire a rifle at other men and could not therefore pretend to the hand of a beautiful Sioux woman with a wooden leg and one of the bravest hearts he had ever known. But that is another story, and these blows to his pride did not in any case cure his foolish romanticism, which was rooted in a distant connection, on his father's side, to Quannah's Comanches.

White Mouse maintained a curiosity about the Asiatic far-travelers and mighty hunters who figured in his ancestry. Four years ago he had lived for a few months among the Asháninka, who, in exchange for beads, shotgun shells and knives, tolerated his filming and note-taking. Now he was back, smiling and waving and bearing a new sack of trade stuff, wanting to know specifically about the hunter's life. Not just to *know*, he declared, but to experience, to *become* a hunter himself. One of his friends from the previous visit, after a shrewd look at the new machete and box of cartridges, agreed to serve as his instructor. This was Carlos, the Small Brown Jaguar.

They waited a few days for a rain to blow through. During this time White Mouse visited several hearths, drank much masato, and worked to remember how to laugh. The procedure was as follows: he came and sat in a palm-thatch hut, where people first greeted, then ignored him. After several minutes of this careful avoidance, a wife would bring a gourd bowl of masato to each man. A few monosyllables were then exchanged. A respectful belching. Another bowl. A little story, perhaps, about the last hunt. Another bowl. After twenty minutes the serious laughter began, a laughter peculiar to the Asháninka, a high, sustained whoop of hilarity that rang clear across the river. Men collapsed backward on grass mats, rolled from side to side, spilled their drink. Sometimes White Mouse had an inkling of the source of this merriment; often he did not, though he entertained the suspicion that he was himself—his great hands and feet and spectacles—often the cause of amusement.

After several bowls of masato, he even felt like playing to this ridicule, as he had seen the Asháninka themselves do when they tripped or bumped into things in the course of the afternoon's revelry. He sang them some of his own native songs: *Comin' 'Round the Mountain, Worried Man Blues,* and *Old MacDonald Had a Farm.* This latter number especially delighted people. The children made him sing it again and again. They loved the ducks and turkeys and tried to learn the words, but always confounded the chorus: here quack, there oink, everywhere a gobble-cluck. White Mouse in his turn grew uproarious at their mishaps, and everyone had a wonderful time.

Then one day the weather improved and Carlos jerked his head toward the mountains and took down his single-shot sixteen gauge. White Mouse, it was agreed, would practice with the bow and arrow. They set off into the trees, bushes, ferns, and creepers, following a trail that was only a foot-wide slot through the green wall. Besides his weapons, White Mouse carried in a shoulder bag a camera, film, cleaning solution for his new contact lenses, spare spectacles, pen, and notebook.

For perhaps two hours, the sun burning ever brighter through the thinning clouds, they walked. Occasionally Carlos halted to listen or utter a bird call, but most of the time he merely moved along, in a fashion that appeared more and more marvelous to White Mouse. The Small Brown Jaguar did not seem to be hurrying at all. He shambled along, pigeon-toed, with the shotgun over his shoulder or at his side, head erect and not apparently watching the trail at all. Without effort he crossed ridge after ridge.

Yet the Mouse, a full head taller than the cat, could not keep up, though he hastened and hurried and hassled without rest. The bow and arrows caught on vines and branches. His running shoes slipped on the wet rocks and roots. The heat was suffocating and sapped his strength. Blinking away sweat, he watched his instructor narrowly, trying to divine his secret. For one thing, bare feet appeared to grip the terrain better. He noted also that

Carlos's toes, never confined, spread very wide. There was something un-
dulating, snake-like, about the shamble, an even glide uphill or down. Try as
he would to imitate this glide, White Mouse ended always in a gasping,
sweating, stumbling, unlovely trot, and he always came last.

When they reached one of the clear, cool rills that trickled down deep,
rocky notches in the mountain's flanks, White Mouse plunged his hands and
arms and face in the water and moaned. Then for a few moments his impres-
sions were sharp and clear: the mighty trunks draped with vines, some as
thick as hawsers; the dense net of blades and thorns and twisted limbs; the
fecund, spongy humus that was itself a miniature jungle where mushroom,
moss, fungus, slug, and ant thrived.

But White Mouse saw these things only fleetingly, for Carlos was ever
impatient to glide onward, so his apprentice had to scramble after, dripping
and muttering. In early afternoon Carlos paused to relieve him of his camera
bag, for the terrain grew steeper. Sometimes they climbed above the clouds
and caught a glimpse of further, higher mountains, dark blue with distance.
Many times the Brown Jaguar darted or drifted from the trail for a few
minutes, whistling or cooing his calls, but returned always empty-handed,
noncommittal. Occasionally he stopped to point at a scuff mark in the mulch
on the forest floor, and uttered names, some of which the White Mouse
knew—pig, deer, tiger—although all the marks except the tiger's looked
the same to him.

When the sun was midway in its fall to the mountain tops, White Mouse
grew afraid. He did not know how many kilometers they had walked in the
last seven hours, but guessed in excess of twenty-five. His legs trembled
and knotted, bringing sharp gasps. There was a fire in his lungs. He was
almost twenty years older than his teacher, and he had spent several of
those years sitting and staring at the pages of books. He stopped more and
more often, covering less and less ground between stops. His own blood-
stream was a continuous thunder in his ears. His thoughts became fragmen-
tary and disconnected, like a dream. He suspected that there were snakes
near, coiled in the leaves.

Carlos turned aside from the trail and pried a roughrinded fruit, like a huge brown hand grenade, from a low palm whose fronds seemed to spray straight from the earth. He popped out the segments with a knife point and cut the top of each segment to reveal five small chambers, containing a mouthful of cool, sweet liquid. After several of these greedy draughts, White Mouse thought himself refreshed. He was also given a stalk from another small plant and instructed to chew it for sustenance. Carlos held his arm up to indicate the angle of the light. *Tarde,* he said, and shook his head. *Tarde.*

They went on, and within a few hundred yards they struck another steep upslope. White Mouse staggered, fell to the ground, and could not seem to get up. His breathing was an insane rasp, in and out, interrupted by occasional bleats. As his vision darkened, he perceived his companion squatting beside him. The Jaguar waited, suppressing a yawn. Finally White Mouse raised his head, whimpering, and the other considered him attentively. Then the Jaguar spoke, a rare occurrence. *"No muere,"* he said. "Not die."

White Mouse considered this advice, grasping finally the real situation, and found it good. He did not want to die ignominiously in the dirt like a foolish, middle-aged romantic. His instructor likewise did not relish packing out a corpse, or even leaving it to rot. Galvanized, the Mouse managed to get to his feet and formulate a question. How far was the nearest house and fire where they could sleep? Carlos puzzled, then arrived at one hand with fingers spread wide. Five kilometers. An uncle, a *kóki,* lived there.

Once erect, White Mouse developed rapidly a system of locomotion, a spare, efficient system which allowed no hazard of fantasy or speculation. Five thousand meters, perhaps six thousand strides. These could be counted. One could take them one at a time. He began, fastening his mind to the count, and only the count, maintaining a pure faith that he would not fall.

After 924 they reached a small creek and White Mouse succeeded in kneeling, rinsing his mouth, and rising. Setting out again, he discovered that he could keep count subliminally as far as 30, freeing his imagination. Perhaps, he allowed himself to hope, Carlos had made a generous estimate. On the other hand, he already knew that a kilometer was an elastic thing to these people; it could stretch as well as contract.

He thought of the march of Progress; each stride a year. He passed the Norman Conquest, the Gutenberg Bible, the Declaration of Independence. Just before he reached the driving of the golden spike to complete the Transatlantic Railroad, he saw something in the gloom ahead. He saw the broad leaves of a banana tree. White Mouse exerted himself not to shake, or cry, and as they approached the bare, packed earth around the thatched hut where dark figures moved about a fire, he even laughed. A loud, long laugh.

After a very brief and perfunctory period of ignoring the newcomers, Kóki laughed too, very happy. He and his wife and seven-year-old boy and new-born girl lived many miles from the river and did not have frequent visitors. The hut had no walls, as is customary in this place, and they could see everything the family owned. Except for two or three aluminum pots, a flour sack, and a hand mirror, everything was of wood or bone or feathers or cotton or gourd. Everyone but the baby girl had bright orange *achiote* smeared on both cheeks, and the woman wore a bunch of parrot feathers on the shoulder of her cushma. She apologized because there was only a little masato, and nothing to eat but a few snails and baked yucca. Kóki, meanwhile, went carefully through their bags and examined everything, as was the custom here. He wondered at the camera, and if the contact lens solution was drinkable.

They began to swill masato instead. Kóki put on his woven headdress with the three-foot bright red feather and took out his wooden flute. He tootled for a while, then grabbed White Mouse by the waist and made him dance. Carlos told the story of the day with many gestures and bird calls, and made Kóki and his wife laugh by relating how White Mouse had walked, fallen, and moaned. White Mouse re-enacted the scene for their amusement, indicating how Carlos had yawned, and they whooped for a long time. Then White Mouse sang Old MacDonald several times. Kóki was so excited he held the Mouse's hand and patted him on the head.

Now and then they took one of the snails from the coals and picked out the steaming meat with a bone splinter, or dipped a chunk of hot yucca in a gourd of salt. White Mouse washed these tidbits down with many bowls of masato, between verses of his song. He recombined the few words he knew

97

into crude sentences: *Good to eat! Snails! I am big! Masato! Good masato! We sing!* He was almost crazy with happiness to be in a place where he could lie down by a fire and merely hold out his bowl to have it filled. And this drink tasted rich and complex and powerful, served to him by Kóki's young, pretty wife. He fell back on the bamboo mat with a wild giggle. White Mouse decided he liked drinking her cool, sweet spit.

Far into the night they celebrated, reeling drunkenly around the fire, laughing themselves into a stupor, playing the flute, and singing. Carlos pointed to a black hole in the cotton scarf of stars in the sky. It was, he said, bitten out by a tiger. White Mouse tried to take out his contacts in the dark and dropped the left one in the dust. On all fours, he howled at the hole in the sky.

Kóki played monkey, imitating this Mouse, with his strange sighs, belches, and a laugh like a snake hissing or a dog barking. With one hand he fondled the Big Mouse face in the dark to know its expression, whether it was asleep yet or still smiling. He whispered in the Mouse ear and put his head on the hairy chest to listen for messages of the heart. He was, he said, the Mouse's uncle too. Still, he could not keep his nephew awake. Mouse went to sleep with the hands still roaming over him, a skull banging into his skull in its enthusiasm, an old song crooning over him.

The next part of the story is about patience. We are not ready yet to reveal how Big White Mouse became father of monkeys, just as two hunters are in no hurry to greet one another, nor is anyone in too much of a rush to drink a few bowls of masato. As the Asháninka say, death comes soon enough; there is no reason to hurry.

The next morning they did not return to the village, as White Mouse had expected. They went on into the forest, higher into the mountains, to the house of Carlos's brother. From there they roamed for some days, traveling with the brother's sons-in-law, young men hungry to hunt. White Mouse discovered that, although he still had difficulty keeping up, he could walk all day without falling down and moaning at sunset. He looked around more, saw more, learned new words. His companions always spotted game first, but they directed him to certain slow-moving birds and squirrels, let him shoot his arrows. Twice he grazed a wing, and before the startled quail could leave its perch Carlos blew it into a cloud of feathers and a soft, tumbling heap.

They politely gave him these birds as if they were his. He plucked the carcasses bare, tied them to his belt with thin vines they pointed out to him, and in camp ceremoniously gave the meat back to his teachers. That, too, was custom. A boy learning to hunt must give away his first half-dozen kills, so he will learn perseverance. White Mouse also plucked and carried the big wild turkeys his friends bagged, and once he gutted and packed a deer. He was delighted to perform these small services, easy for one of his bulk, in exchange for his instruction and the meat and masato given him each evening. Also—it had become a ritual—he would sing Old MacDonald every night, and now a few of the children had mastered some verses and sang with him.

One day Kóki and his family came into camp bringing Carlos's wife and two sons, so with the other brother and two married daughters and all their children there were twenty or more people around several fires. To feed so many it was necessary to hunt seriously every day. The women went out with baskets to gather snails, and sometimes they traveled some way with the hunters, a few children in tow as well.

White Mouse had to laugh at himself to see how Carlos's wife, five feet tall and six months pregnant with a big basket tumplined from her brow, navigated easily the very trails where he had thought he would expire. Some of the boys eight and ten, dirty cushmas flapping like bat wings, also flew up and down the mountainside where he had only days before staggered and cried out. He could understand at last how these people had made their way from Siberia to Greenland, from Saskatchewan to the Mojave, from Cape Cod to the Everglades, from Oaxaca to the Cordilleras to the Amazon to Tierra del Fuego, from ice cap to ice cap. They simply glided, in no hurry, stopping in delight over a stray snail or a fresh tiger track.

The journey took ten thousand years. It required patience. White Mouse observed examples of this virtue, chief among which was the long afternoon spent killing a *tsamíri,* one of the four kinds of turkey, a big one that took refuge high in a giant pentandra tree after Carlos broke its wing. The bird was perhaps a hundred feet up, and the shells lacked the authority to reach it (the Peruvian government limits the powder and shot load of cartridges available to the public). Andrés, a son-in-law who accompanied them, had five arrows and White Mouse had three. At full draw, an arrow had force enough to drive through the tsamíri. But the bird hunkered on a branch amid fairly thick cover, so a marksman had to try to thread the shaft through leaves and random vines, aiming also into bright sun.

For an hour they shot one barrage after another, listening as each shaft whipped through the foliage in its arc back to earth. Inevitably, they lost the arrows one by one: some stuck in the branches aloft, others vanished in the dense undergrowth. White Mouse tried to aim carefully, and once a shot sped true, but he had achieved care at the expense of reducing his draw a bit, so the arrow merely tapped the bird on the chest, its power exhausted, and fell back. His companions whooped merrily at this turn of events, and whooped again when Andrés, with his smooth, sudden draw and soft release, twice nicked feathers from the tail.

Finally Andrés had but two arrows and White Mouse had none. For another thirty minutes they watched while the pair of shafts hissed into the tree and dropped back clean, waited while Andrés ferreted them out and resumed his firing position. White Mouse wondered at the efficiency of this strategy, speculated on the return in protein for such an expenditure of time and energy. But finally an arrow flew perfectly, touching not a twig or leaf before it spiked the turkey through the breast. The great wings spread and flapped in surprise; the body tilted, cartwheeled off the branch, flopped perhaps eight or ten feet and then hung upside down, the wings still beating feebly, fouled somehow in a branch.

White Mouse's cry of relief and triumph died on his lips. Carlos and Andrés whooped in joy. Another defeat! How delightful! They began to shake

100

the thickest vines, hoping to dislodge their quarry. White Mouse helped them, swinging like Tarzan on a three-inch cable, howling his frustration. For half an hour they kept up this sport, until their arms were sore from the yanking and whipping back and forth. Andrés tried his last arrow and it stuck high in the trees. Surely now they would quit, White Mouse thought. The sun was almost at the ridgetop and they were miles from home.

But when he looked again Andrés had cut a long strip of tough bark from a sapling. With the bark he hobbled himself, linking his ankles perhaps a foot apart. Then he hopped to another tree, a very slim and very tall tree perhaps fifty feet away from the big pentandra. He began to climb, gripping and hoisting with his arms, his weight acting to brace his bound feet against the trunk. He went up perhaps twenty yards without stopping, rested briefly, then made another ten, bringing him to a point opposite the dangling bird. There he rested again, calling down to Carlos, the two of them laughing.

He proceeded to break out sections of branch and strip off their leaves, making clubs some three feet long, which he hurled at the bird in the neighboring tree. To take aim, however, he had to balance on narrow branches, hanging by one hand and throwing with the other in an attempt to whirl the club through a narrow avenue in the foliage. Below, the other two watched and waited, occasionally pulling on a vine to set the dead bird swaying. Six clubs. Ten clubs. Eighteen clubs. Twenty-one clubs.

When the last sunlight was caught in the treetops where he worked, Andrés struck the tsamíri and it tumbled over one branch, then another, and plummeted to earth. The hunter came after, sliding down the trunk in a spray of bark dust to the ground littered now with feathers and broken branches. He was grinning like a demon. White Mouse hurried to secure the heavy bird in a length of vine and sling it from his shoulder. The firm of Plucker and Packer, he thought to himself, tired and happy. They glided down the trail and he guessed the long effort was worth it, since with the masato there would now be quite a story.

Their best day, the monkey day, began with the killing of two more turkeys. These birds, weighing between six and twelve pounds, were black with white and gray trim, difficult to see in the crisscrossing shadows of the jungle. They could race along the ground or fly into the tops of great trees. When Carlos or Andrés found one they stalked it with a swift tenacity that amazed White Mouse as much as their shambling glide on the trail. Whistling at the bird to maintain contact, they crouched and wormed through the labyrinthine undergrowth, appearing briefly in one opening and then—How? Covering such distance in so little time?—reappearing in another.

The first two monkeys were handled much differently. As soon as they heard the squeak and chatter, Carlos and Andrés set up a racket of their own. They clamped leaves between their lips and made perfectly the sucking kiss sound, and they broke off branches and switched them against tree trunks. Carlos waved high one of the bright red shotgun shells.

White Mouse watched intently and soon he saw the antic pair skittering through the branches overhead. They were very small, smaller than the turkeys, with long, questionmark tails. The tiny faces seemed ancient, framed by beard and brow the color of frost. They peered and gesticulated with nervous hands, shrieked, hopped and swung nearer. Soon they were no more than twenty feet away, directly above. Carlos sucked at his leaf. Andrés, eyes glittering, slid an arrow across the bow and hooked it on the string.

One of the monkeys paused, sat upright on a branch. Andrés bent the bow, held, released. The arrow darted up like a swallow and with a sound like a sudden, sharp sigh, impaled the monkey. She was instantly excited, gyrating around the shaft, fondling it anxiously, squealing. The red spike protruding from her back clattered clumsily in the branches.

Her mate grew frantic. He raced higher in the tree, returned, plucked urgently at her shoulder, shrieked in her ear. But she grew more and more preoccupied with the stake driven through her, dragging it this way and that along the branch. Andrés waited until her fretful mate hesitated beside her, then drew again, released, and the second arrow slanted up, slowed into his flesh, stopping halfway through. Now he too spun in irritation and surprise, forgetting her as she had forgotten him, and the hunters below laughed uproariously at this demonstration of inconstant fidelity.

The death-dance went on and on, the monkeys chattering less but active still in picking and wrenching at the wicked skewers that robbed them of mobility and grace. The hunters' amusement ebbed at last, so Andrés clambered into the tree and threw the small, squirming bodies to the ground. Carlos recovered them, gripped them by the neck and pulled out the bloody shafts. Holding each firmly against a log, he pressed with a hard thumb under the matchstick ribs, until the little walnut skulls turned aside, teeth bared, and the bodies began to spasm.

When both lay limp in the grass, White Mouse was handed a large leaf and a length of vine to wrap them in. But he seemed reluctant, and his companions remarked it. These *tsítsi* look like children, he said. Carlos ran a finger along the Mouse's forearm, saying, You are hairy like they are. Perhaps this is my son, my daughter, White Mouse said and attempted a careless smile. The others laughed loud at this possibility. Yes, they said, your son. Carry him home. We will roast him and eat him.

They headed back by another trail, and before long they heard a rustling in the treetops some distance into the forest. Andrés produced a little bamboo whistle and blew on it, producing a chortling call. Something answered, so they crouched under a tree and called again. After a time the chortling was quite near, and White Mouse saw finally the dark, rangy forms pouring through the high branches. *Oshtéro*, the spider monkey, with long, crooked black arms and hooking tail. They were much larger than the tsítsi, and much more circumspect, moving like liquid shadows.

Carlos and Andrés were alert, thrilled. They slipped away after the band of monkeys, darting so quickly through the brush that White Mouse soon lost sight of them. In a while he heard a shot, far away, so he sat down to wait, having nothing to do but brush ants away from the little leaf package of meat. When his companions returned they were dragging a big female

103

by her long arms. More of your relatives, they said to White Mouse. A too-curious woman. They seemed quietly elated. There would be plenty to eat for everybody on this day. As there were no more cartridges and the shadows were long again, they set off homeward.

In laughing deference to the Mouse's sensibilities, they did not make him pack his big relative. Andrés lashed her knees to her elbows, and with a loop of the tough bark slung her on his shoulders, so that she faced back down the trail. White Mouse, coming behind, often caught her nodding stupidly at him, her lower lip drooling blood. One forearm was lashed in such a way that her leathery palm seemed raised in hearty farewell.

They reached camp after sundown and threw the carcasses on a woven grass mat by the hearth. Then they dropped themselves on the split bamboo platform with sighs of luxurious fatigue. The women hurried to bring bowls of masato, freshly made, and to build up the fires. Three young men from another camp a few kilometers away had stopped by for the night, and these newcomers inquired eagerly about the hunt, the three monkeys, and the immense, silent white man. Carlos began the tale, which recalled exactly the wanderings of the morning. He repeated the calls of the birds and monkeys, gestured to indicate their direction. There were digressions on various subjects, some frivolous, and much banter back and forth.

Squatting or lounging on the platform, their earth-colored cushmas drawn about them and slashes of orange paint on their cheeks, this group of men looked like a flock of voluble roosting birds to the Mouse. He could not follow most of the jokes, but joined into the whooping occasionally. Soon enough, he knew, it would be time for his song. Meanwhile he watched as the women heated a huge aluminum pot of water. When it was steaming, Carlos's wife seized the big spider by one arm and leg and dunked her head-down in the pot. A little girl had brought a candle and in its flickering light he saw the knife peeling away the black fur, revealing a little ivory doll's head and pathetically shrunken shoulders.

The recounting of the hunt had now involved White Mouse, who was being examined by the newcomers. They insisted he stand back-to-back with them, to demonstrate his great height, and hold up his wide paws against their small slender hands. With his limited stock of words and much miming he told them how he was good and they were good and the masato was good, how he had panted and Carlos had yawned, how they had shot arrow after arrow at the wounded tsamíri. These tales were well received, and when without thinking he let a resounding fart there was general, enthusiastic acclaim.

Andrés reminded him to tell of his son and daughter. This anecdote made White Mouse the center of affectionate attention. He was urged to reveal the dense pelt under his shirt front. The men gathered to tug at the hair here and also on his forearms. Indeed, they said, he must be related to tsítsi and oshtéro, and soon he could have his son and daughter for dinner. They pointed and White Mouse saw that the two small monkeys, blackened and shriveled, reclined on a frame of green branches above one smoking fire. By another, Carlos's woman had exposed with her blade a pale, skimbleshanks adolescent girl with the head of a Moorish dwarf. Jerked by knife strokes, the head seemed to nod to him.

Everyone drank more *masato,* snacking also on the snails. It took a certain trick with the bone splinter to hook out the spiral of soft, streaming meat. There was much laughing now, much silliness, more farting. Young men went off to secure bigger logs and build the fires higher, for on those ridges in the winter season nights are very cool. Kóki and another young man tootled on their flutes, and soon the children gathered around the Mouse to beg for their favorite song.

The Mouse had drunk a very great deal, like the other men, so he lay flat on his back on the platform and sang loudly to the roof. Over and over he built up to the quack-quacks and oink-oinks, but except for Carlos's elder son no one could get them anywhere near straight, and as he had at last begun to understand, this was the right approach, for among these people nothing was so humorous as failure.

He was roused finally and presented with a tiny forearm, hand still attached, smoked to a crisp. There was an expectant pause, and all the

106

brown, open faces with solid white teeth bared in a grin were turned to him. He pretended to demur and they whooped. He accepted the arm and they whooped even louder. He tasted and frowned, rolled his eyes, began at last to chew mournfully, and the laughter came rolling over him like a waterfall. There goes your son, they called to him. Your daughter is next.

White Mouse laughed too, and as long as he did not watch the boys cracking the little skull and using its curved sections to spoon out two or three bites of brain, he even enjoyed the meat moderately, though it was dark and had an odd scent. After his meal he drank and sang and laughed until he fell asleep, was awakened and caroused some more, then fell asleep again on mats thrown down before the fire. The newcomers were given the honor of sleeping curled against him, their feet almost in the coals, and throughout the night they murmured laughter or fragments of his song into his ear.

White Mouse slept well, not tormented with foolish, romantic dreams. He knew he was only a plucker and packer, and would never be a true hunter, but his failure was also fun. These people would bring him meat, perhaps merely because he was large and hairy and would sing. They were also polite and would not let him die in the dirt from his awkwardness. They ignored his arrival; they would ignore his departure; in between everyone would drink a lot and have a good time.

A few weeks later, waiting in the village for the little plane to come, he heard the children on their way to school. They were singing.

> Odd MicDunow ed a furm
> Ee-yi ee-yi yooo

The voices were pure and thoughtless. He saw the small figures filing through the trees, cushmas fluttering, cotton shoulderbags stuffed with books. Unlike their parents, they could read and write.

> Addonis furm ed a dock,
> Ee-yi ee-yi yooo!

107

He thought of the plane that would come, of the other planes that flew over, bearing the Japanese and their survey instruments or the soldiers, of the road that was being built into the village.

> Widda quick-quock air
> Ana quick-quock dare . . .

He was all at once sad and afraid. Many, many people were coming this way; people who no longer hunted or believed in hunting or understood other people who did. Then in another instant he thought of how he must learn to laugh, no matter what, even sad and afraid. This at least he could learn from them. This at least he could take away.

> Ana quick-a-quick quock
> Air-dare quock-a-quock . . . oink . . .

The voices dissolved into giggles, growing fainter, and then he heard the distant, mosquito-like drone of the approaching airplane.

SOURDOUGHS, FILIBUSTERS, & A ONE-EARED MULE

They were called sourdoughs presumably because they once baked their own bread and biscuits in the rough camps of the Yukon. Thirty years ago, in their last days, those who escaped the nursing home probably survived on Campbell's soup and potato chips. Anyway, a more accurate designation would have made reference to their tobacco-stained beards or wide, union-label suspenders that held up trousers of canvas or heavy twill. One loop of those suspenders generally secured a fob of plaited leather which was used to hoist from its pocket a Waltham railroad timepiece. This instrument, of stainless steel with one glass side, was the size of a flattened turkey egg, and audible at seven paces even inside the pocket. Its weight might have unbalanced the more dessicated of these gents but for their logger boots, which anchored them securely to earth. With such counterweights they had no need of canes and could drink a good deal without fear of tipping over.

They lived in various more or less permanent habitats. Shanties by the tracks in small western towns. Rooming houses and hotels for transients. A dilapidated farmhouse, left untended by some prosperous relatives. Occasionally, an old truck. Wherever they hung their hats, they lived alone, for they were alternately taciturn and garrulous, usually cranky and sometimes downright mean.

Most of them received small checks from the government, payment for service in a great war or merely for having survived under any circumstances for so long. They did not need much. They were bachelors, with no

109

dependents. Their tools were simple and would last the rest of their lives: a bone-handled claspknife; a tin box containing buttons, shoelaces, bolts, and screws; small bottles of aspirin, bicarbonate, and epsom salts; a straight razor (long unused), and a few old photographs. There was usually a duffel bag or battered suitcase, a kettle and skillet and iron spoon, a shovel, double-bitted axe, and perhaps a shotgun. The most independent and prosperous might even own a vehicle, usually a Model A pickup half as old as they were.

Gas-powered transportation meant that a sourdough had probably not yet emerged from his larval phase as a prospector. For what sourdoughs had in common, above and beyond trivial matters of dress and demeanor, was firsthand experience in the grand and fateful enterprise of the white man in the Americas: the search for mineral wealth in the guts of the earth. First gold and silver, then lead and copper, finally oil and uranium. Most of these materials were found in the mountainous regions of the West, from the Sierra Madre to the Yukon, in the deepest, most desolate heart of the wilderness. They were unearthed by men often described as stark mad by the aborigines whose territories the prospectors infested like a cloud of locusts; lunatics who would suffer any extreme of hunger, thirst, fire, or flood, undergo any hardship, forsake any allegiance, risk any fate—torture, death, dishonor—for the mere chance—a very slim chance it was, too—of spying in their pans a few flecks of shining metal.

These were the authentic prospectors, who might or might not make themselves subsequently into miners. For the pure type was usually not interested in developing his claim, in achieving dynastic wealth, the authority of high office, and the admiration of subsequent generations. The true prospector was interested in panning out those flecks of light, stuffing them in his little deerskin poke, and moving further up the creek with a fire gnawing at his heart as if it were a smoldering stump. He would squint up the draw, watching for an outcrop with a streak of white quartz, or scan a rocky stream bed for signs of float ore. He would dig at a likely spot with the controlled frenzy of a fox after a mole. If he struck a rich placer gravel or a vein he would build a sluice box or rocker and strip enough high-grade stuff to make a mule grunt when the paniers were heaved onto the pack frame; and then he rode hard to a railhead where he could walk into a bank or a store or a saloon and tell the wealthiest, most important man in town that he'd better find a chair and sit down and listen, real hard, if he had the sense God gave a fencepost.

Or if he were a prospector of the absolute purest and highest type, he would simply stride into the biggest saloon on the street and throw one of the pokes on the counter, saying, "Bartender, take enough out'n that to stand these poor bastards a drink," or even—skipping several convivial steps—"Any of you egg-suckin' stove-up bullsnappers got enough gumption to git off yer tails an' do some ridin' I'll show you a goddamn mountain of this color. Locatin' fee is two hunnert dollars apiece cash money, laid out on this bar tomorry mornin'."

After certain transactions over the next few days or weeks, the pure prospector will proceed to diffuse his profits into the community, purchasing the highest available class of goods: women, whiskey, cigars, personal finery, horses, and friends, in that order. His claims will have passed of course into the hands of neat, abstemious men who will hire engineers and freight in steam engines, iron pipe, dynamite, and smelter brick; a little later they will build a railroad, incorporate the boom town, sell plats, and get themselves elected to Congress. By this time the pure prospector will likely be broke, cadging drinks from unwary greenhorns trapped in his garrulous, self-aggrandizing narratives. If he lingers to perfect this art, he has begun the transformation into a certified sourdough. But he may talk his way into another grubstake, sober up, assemble pick, shovel, pan, bedroll, and mule, and vanish again into the mountains—the Sawatch, Medicine Bow, Absaroka, Bitterroot, or Selkirk Range—looking for that tiny glitter in the pan on some creek that will wind up with a name like Bonanza, Highgrade, Lucky or Silver Dollar; or perhaps Hardscrabble, Suicide, Bitch, Shirttail, or the legendary Shit Creek.

These improvident if not demented toilers remain for the most part nameless or receive a single mention as the locators of lodes that made the fortunes of an aristocracy—the Hearsts, Dalys, and Guggenheims. To earn this dubious glory they endured privations scarcely imaginable. They lived for years on beans and sowbelly, with potatoes soaked in vinegar as vitamin supplement and mummified apricots for dessert. They crossed Chilkoot Pass in the dead of winter, drowned horses in the spring flood of the Salmon, left their scalps to adorn the teepees of Lakota chiefs. Day in and day out they stood knee-deep in ice water, prey for voracious mosquitoes, performing a tedious and backbreaking labor to earn the few dollars it took to keep them alive.

They did their work well, fanning out into the wilderness, picking and panning in every spur, gully, and spring on the continent; and whenever they found something, their laggard fellows poured in at their heels by the thousands, then tens of thousands, and finally millions. These following legions cut the forests, diverted the rivers, exterminated the Indians, fenced in great herds of cattle, laid the rails, built the grand mansions, and pronounced the grand phrases to glorify the whole enterprise. Their temples were Skagway, Lewiston, Butte, Boise, Cheyenne, Denver, San Francisco, Santa Fe, El Paso. For of course the most cunning of the lot realized early that there was more wealth in the pockets of the onrushing multitudes than in the hardrock high country, that a few wornout oxen bought cheap or a wagonload of seed or a sawmill could be parlayed into a fortune, that the new centers of "civilization" springing up overnight, almost miraculously, were more powerful and durable than bullion from the mines they were created to serve. At the same time, none of this power could be released without the glitter in the bowels of the mountain. They might not have expressed it so, but they all knew that gold is a talisman of profound power and mystery. They knew it even from common folklore: the tales of the Goose, the Fleece, El Dorado, King Midas, the Rainbow. We have no comparable myths of lead, or legends of molybdenum. It is gold that galvanizes men to supernatural feats of endurance, enterprise, and courage; or, alternately, drives them to the most violent despair.

The first of the stories I can remember was of this latter variety. My own father related it about his father, who lived in that crucial period of transition from prospector to sourdough, so the tale had from the beginning an elegiac flavor. Grandfather first drifted into Idaho following the Thunder Mountain boom, a late silver strike of very modest proportions, mostly memorable today as the backdrop for a Zane Grey novel. When he couldn't locate decent ore, Grandfather homesteaded a little jackpine slope and cattle pasture, which, almost as an afterthought, he populated with a wife and seven children. In the early years, between roundups, he kept up his assessment work on a claim in the Deadwood country, where a man could pick up galena float almost anywhere, and made a few extra dollars packing supplies to the handful of miners still hanging on in that region. It was on one of these routine journeys that he encountered the odd case which became a family legend, a sort of moral summary of an age.

The parable was colored thoughout by my father's particular style, and to get the effect of it you have to imagine a narrator who advances without perceivable plan, without the slightest notion of structure or design to delineate one story from another; who interrupts the line of action to clean his fingernails with a pocket knife or his ears with a matchstick; who digresses into tirades against large companies and distant politicians or argues with his listeners over the precise date and locale of each event—whether, for example, the road from Yellow Pine (which has no purpose in this tale except to carry Grandfather to his dramatic encounter with the old miner) was built before or after the landslide at Warren which buried a man, the brother—or was it?—of a sheepherder nicknamed the Ox, whose legendary feats of strength could at this point upsurp Grandfather entirely and become the featured anecdote for the evening, unless one rapt soul (the youngest, always myself) should blurt out the question and reminder—"But Dad, what about *Grandpa* and the old guy who almost died?"—and receive for his pains a look of mild yet monumental scorn as preface to an interminable, devious return to the original story, to Grandfather still riding with his packstring along the wagon road from Yellow Pine, hooves thudding dully in earth damp from spring runoff, riding now in shadow, for the sun is behind the ridge.

I knew what Grandpa was about to find. There was no suspense. My father most often introduced a tale against all the accumulated tradition of skilled bards, from Homer to Hammett, revealing the climax baldly enough in his first line.

"Just like the time," he would say, "Dad found that old sonofabitch with his throat cut."

One elbow propped on the faded oilcloth atop the table, his stockinged feet on a chair drawn up beside the kitchen stove, he would have been reminded by something someone else said—his brother or one of the sawyers or cat drivers or old Chet who came to play chess or even my mother, who worked circumspectly a few steps away at the sink—some account of one of life's grisly little ironies, some misguided fatalism, or merely a reference to violent surprise. Any of these could suggest this classic tale, which would then, in its clarity and perfection, supplant and represent all rivals.

But the matter did not unfold so directly. "Waldo," my mother might first interject, her voice gentle yet containing something of the manner of a snap shot from a running horse. The intonation of this word was complex, an absent-minded resignation and reproach. On the surface it meant she was doing the dishes while my father was only talking. At a deeper level it meant his swearing still made her suffer, after a dozen years, and suffer even more now because I was still allegedly a child, sitting on the floor with my back to the woodbox where I could see and hear everything.

My father might hesitate, waving vaguely at his ear as if a fly had approached too near. "Should have rode right on by," he would continue then. "Anybody that goddamned dumb."

"Hell, Dad didn't know nobody was a-goin' to be such a damn fool," my uncle might observe, referring of course to the old miner. My uncle and my father drew out and provoked each other's stories by a contrariness that ranged all the way from rhetorical remonstrance to a profane shouting that drove my mother, white-lipped, from the room. On rare occasions a chair would be thrown aside and a door slammed on the way out.

If an adult who had not heard the story was present, he or she might inquire straightforwardly about this gruesome incident. Apparently surprised at such ignorance, Waldo would frown and feign a direct assault on his subject, beginning with some necessary facts.

"Well, dad was freightin' grub and supplies—a little kerosene and a few nails and laundry soap and the like—to these old sourdoughs—bunch of old daralicks is what they was—who was holed up there on the Deadwood—this was 'fore they built the dam—"

"Not a whole hell of a lot afore," my uncle would object.

"They started on that dam the summer of 1906. I've heard dad say that a thousand times. You was too little to know."

"You better clean them ears out again, then, because he told me he run the dragline on the road in there the year I was born and that's 1905 or else my goddamn birth certificky is cockeyed."

"It ain't the only thing cockeyed about you."

"But tell about the *old man!*" I might burst in, fearful that if I did not control them the story would disintegrate into meaningless controversy. Not that sometimes these sparring matches weren't diverting—when the contestants were in form their combat was fascinating beyond anything of substance in what they said. Their epithets alone could dazzle me or send me into paroxysms of suffocated giggling, though I was forbidden, with unusual gravity, to repeat them.

"Him?" Waldo once said about a man whom my mother had mentioned with approval, a young man who wore a tie and came to our house with a briefcase. "That shithouse mouse?" Every time I thought of this fabulous creature the muscles in my abdomen spasmed, for I could see the young man tremendously reduced, his whiskered nose twitching, a pink tail emerging from his tiny coat, as he scampered through a crack in the boards of the outhouse. Even years later, when I encountered a certain furtive, slightly unsavory attitude, the phrase would pop into mind and cause me to choke on my gin.

Still, my instinct then was not for brilliant, scatological stichomythia, but for larger patterns. I had noticed that even after many tellings my father would sometimes recall a new detail that would give an additional touch of color or drama to events, and I made it my duty to gather all such details and supply them if he hesitated. There was of course the risk of the final, magisterial dismissal ("Hell, boy, you wasn't even *born* then"), but the reward was a tale that grew richer—more graphic, more complex.

It occurred to Waldo once, for example, that one of the mules, a big black animal named Tarbaby, would get so obstreperous on the trail that Granddad would have to unpack him—clear down to his hide—and load him back up again before going on; and it seemed possible, even likely since other speculations remained yet more tenuous, that Tarbaby's orneriness had decided Grandfather to turn off on the trail to the old man's diggings.

It was known that there was no special motive for the visit. When Granddad had specific orders he delivered them, but he might also drop off an occasional letter or package, or pull in to check a loose cinch or shoe, or simply feel like a little talk. He was not, as I understood it, given to a lot of conversation, but he doubtless knew the value of words, however few and commonplace, in that country. After Thunder Mountain slid into a creek, damming it and putting the camp four fathoms under, the hardluck miners scrambled out into the remotest draws where they could dig only during the swift four months of summer. The other eight were buried under as many feet of snow, and alone for so long in a cabin three strides by four, surrounded by silent whiteness, the most taciturn of men could develop an ungovernable yearning for the sound of a human voice, for the simple ephemeral pleasure of shooting the breeze.

So for some such reason or medley of them Grandpa took the fork into the old man's claim, hurrying probably because he wanted to reach Stoley meadows before dark and camp by himself where the pasture was easy. He would have paused at the edge of the meadow by the creek to let the mules stamp and blow and would have remarked that no smoke came from the cabin chimney. Looking uphill toward the little heap of tailings, he would find no sign of movement there. Why he elected to ford the creek anyway, to draw near enough to verify with a halloo that the place was deserted, no man knows. Perhaps the emptiness, the silence, when he expected to hear the rumble of the raster, made Granddad uneasy; or the absence of the miner's workhorse, even though there was no fresh dung on the trail. In any case he was probably unconsciously listening for a distant whinny, or the sound of an axe, or even a shot—the fool hens and blue grouse were everywhere in June—when he heard the moans from the cabin.

The workhorse and the raster just thrown down there a few lines back surely need a little explanation, for the crude methods of the independent miner, before electricity and internal combustion, have long been forsaken. They also can widen the scope of this investigation to take in those more ancient gold fields to the south, whose history is if anything more lurid and spooky than our own, and also to pay some tribute to the nameless and uncelebrated beasts of burden who provided the raw power for the whole tragic enterprise. For the Spaniard and his horse throw a long shadow across both Americas.

What my grandfather called a raster was a primitive device for crushing ore, the word being derived from the Spanish *arrastrar*, "to drag, to trail along." The device consisted of a deck of low, flat boulders several feet across. In the center of this deck the miner sank a post with a socket drilled in its top end. He set an iron pin in the socket, anchored vertically but free to turn. To the pin was bolted a crossbar with arms of uneven length. A granite boulder the size of a bushel basket was attached by means of a length of chain to the short arm, and a horse was harnessed to the longer one. As the horse plodded around the deck, the boulder was dragged over it, around and around, so that the chunks of ore thrown on the flat stone surface were slowly ground to powder, which could then be washed in a pan to concentrate the gold-bearing sand. Quicksilver applied to the concentrate extracted the gold, which was recovered then by retorting—driving off the mercury as fumes.

A rude system, but an improvement over the first methods devised in the mines of Peru and Mexico. There the enterprising conquistador had two sources of power, the mule and the Indian. Both were harnessed for a short lifetime in large-scale, wasteful operations whose aim was very simply to refine the greatest possible quantity of gold and silver in the shortest possible time and ship it to Spain, where the king could spend it on frescoes and foreign wars.

Smaller and wirier than a mule, the Indian was sent down the shaft and through the drift tunnels to dig the ore and haul it out on his back. He worked in dust and by the light of torches, so one of the last uncertainties of his existence was the question of whether he would die of silicosis or monoxide poisoning. For his fellows, mule drivers in the rasting pits, there was no such variety. In these shallow rock-lined pits the mules were hitched directly to the boulders, and all ingredients—ore, water, and mercury—were heaved in after them. The Indians drove the mules back and forth through this poisonous mulch day after day, month after month, but not for many years. The hooves rotted off the mule and the man lost his hair in the first year or two. When the mercury reached the cartilage in their joints, convulsions set in, followed soon by paralysis or gibbering insanity. Four years was considered a very long time to persist at this employment. For the select few given the lighter task of roasting concentrate to remove the quicksilver, life was even shorter, for the fumes from this operation were the deadliest of all.

The burros—and their more aristocratic relatives, the horses—proved hardy and fertile enough to survive these hardships. A little more than a hundred years after Cortés, we have record of ranches that boasted forty thousand head of stock. Of the Indians, conversely, only a few escaped in significant numbers. There were two basic strategies: the Tarahumara—so tough and primitive that they did not even ambush deer with bow and arrow but preferred to run them down on foot—retreated into caves deep in the stupendous canyons of Chihuahua, where (as we shall see) a few are still to be found; the Apache chose to interfere directly with the great business of Spanish civilization—the extraction of mineral wealth—and these spectacular raiders succeeded by exploiting in their own terms the boon of the new herds. They mastered the horse as few others have and used it to steal more horses, earning within two generations a mournful compliment from an official reporting from the field to the vice-regent. These savages, he wrote, launched their mounted attacks "in better order and with more skill than the Spanish soldier."

The ferocity of the Apache is a commonplace legend and often decried by the early chroniclers. Their appetite for horses and revenge was gargantuan, and they made the arts, sciences, and commerce very risky and sporadic indeed on the northern frontier of the empire. The example was not lost on other tribes, who occasionally revolted from the alternative of slavery and slow poisoning. In 1644, for example, the Tobosos ran off with thirty-five hundred head of mules and cattle in a single raid on the settlement of Indé, and left numerous headless conquerors in their wake.

But however daring and swift this American mongol cavalry, they had little chance to prevail against the encroaching whites. They did not understand the sinister power of gold. Fast ponies, plenty of game, good water and grass, an occasional venture against an enemy—usually to steal horses or women—these were the things of interest to the unsophisticated savage. He certainly did not contemplate brigandage on the scale being developed by the Europeans.

The English and French crowns, for example, quickly saw the advantage of simply relieving the Spaniards of the gold the latter had just robbed—at great pain and expense—from the Incas and Aztecs. No need to mine, haul, and smelt. The buccaneers put in a few hours with cannon and cutlass and came away with pure ingots. Soon enough they saw the additional advantage of stealing the whole northern continent and sending their own subjects and slaves to occupy it. These deportees, however, eventually caught on to the game and stole the continent for themselves—keeping the slaves, who had finally only their own persons to make off with, everything else of value having been already confiscated.

The latter half of the last century was the great age of imaginative robbery, expedited by the locomotive, steamship, international bank, and repeating rifle. Between the Mexican and the Spanish-American wars, a little over fifty years, the Yanks, as they had come to be known, took the western

119

regions; they settled California, Nevada, Utah, Arizona, New Mexico, Texas, Hawaii, Alaska, and Puerto Rico, and briefly invaded Mexico, Nicaragua, and Cuba.

Gold served actually and metaphorically as the agent of all this rapid, headlong change. For simple and practical men, it was a matter of laying hands on the raw stuff, for with a few sacks of dust one could acquire what he needed: a farm, a store, a wife, livestock, or drygoods. On more complex, visionary personalities, gold operated alchemically: it transmuted them into seekers of glory, taught them that mere bullion was not the goal, but rather the quest itself, an endless, incandescent quest which could bind men together in the deepest of brotherhoods or in the direst treachery, but which in any case entailed ecstasies and agonies that eventually rendered ordinary life flat and unbearable. Gold is nothing much in itself, a lump of too-soft metal with an agreeable sheen, but as an idea, a principle of indomitable aspiration with an accompanying thrill of hazard, it is perhaps the most powerful magic on earth.

This dimension of gold explains why some men, as soon as they obtained it, gambled to parlay their stake into iron, coal, copper, oil, railroads, real estate, hog bellies, textiles, whatever, and then used these resources to buy political office or influence with which, in turn, further invasions and conquests could be launched. It also explains why other men fell into a bottomless existential gloom relieved only by bouts of dissipation or the most outrageous, quixotic, and hopeless acts.

Grandfather must have known he was dealing with the dark side of the magic metal even before he pushed or kicked aside the door of the cabin and saw the dried blood everywhere, inhaled the stench of it, located the shrunken and ravaged figure in the bunk. What he thought then, in the first few seconds after these perceptions, was a matter of eternal speculation for my father, my uncle, and various transient auditors. Surely foul play was possible. Every mining camp in the West had its share of gory legends, usually based squarely on fact. Shootouts, bushwhackings, necktie parties, and knifeplay were the classics, but occasionally there were imaginative innovations: a Chinaman or Siwash set on fire and turned loose to provide a moving target; a flatcar loaded with dynamite and dispatched into a mill as discouragement to scab labor. The harsh, monotonous life of the mining camps seemed to provoke violent adventures and diversions.

For the moment, as the tale came down to me, Grandfather had to put aside his curiosity and busy himself to maintain the faint spark of life in the old prospector. The wound in his throat was terrible, though miraculously not fatal, but there was nothing in the tiny cabin to serve as a remedy. The place was a boar's nest of filthy clothing, emptied tins, broken tack, and tools—all the rank debris of male solitude. Grandfather had to clean a pot, fill it at the creek, and build a fire to boil water. He tore up one of Grandmother's dishtowels for bandages and a washcloth to tidy up. Doubtless he made some kind of tea, perhaps laced with a little of the whiskey that packers normally carried as an all-purpose disinfectant and restorative. My father was most certain about the irritation Granddad felt at seeing the light dying red on the eastern ridge, for it meant he would have to stay the night, which meant he would also have to unpack the mules and turn them into the corral without forage.

Sixty years earlier, nameless tens of thousands like these two marginal operators launched the great rush to California. Many of them were mustered out of the army after the Mexican campaigns, and came west with this experience still fresh in their memories, into the new territories which were the main booty of that war. What they found, for the most part, was torment and disillusionment. If they managed to cross the salt flats of Utah and the barren expanse of the Humboldt basin, they found the Sierra foothills crawling with ill-prepared, inexperienced, and desperate men like themselves. Hovels were thrown up along every creek, scanty supplies freighted in at scarcely credible prices, the countryside ransacked for every scrap of firewood and food. The cattle and orchards of Sutter's hacienda were devoured in the first wave, his house—the finest in the state—burned to the ground, his Indian serfs driven off or killed. No one cared. Previous "rights,"

"titles," "property" were meaningless. Immediate possession was all: the stake in the ground, the pan in the creek, gold in the pocket.

The main tale has been told often enough. What concerns us here is the astounding durability of dreams born from the rumor of gold, despite the suffering of the average forty-niner. The visionaries, as we have said, took a bold step beyond the mere yellow stuff. In the seething drama of westward movement they saw the outline of empire, a high destiny, the context for magnificent deeds. They saw also great numbers of restless, unscrupulous men whose lust for wealth went unslaked, men hardened by adversity, no strangers to violence, reckless for any adventure that might revive the dream. Many had some experience fighting "greasers" or Indians or each other, and almost all felt cheated of the riches they had come so far to find. To the visionaries, this horde of reckless riffraff was an immense resource.

There were other powerful currents running in the land at this time. The Missouri Compromise was unraveling, and armed skirmishes between free-soilers and the pro-slavery faction had broken out in Kansas. The industrial nations of Western Europe were zealously pursuing new colonies in Asia, Africa, the Caribbean, and the South Pacific, while struggling to suppress revolutionary movements within their own borders. The United States was alarmed at British and French aspirations in Canada, Mexico, and Central America, and had therefore revived the Monroe Doctrine with considerable truculence.

This cauldron of greed and xenophobia produced the filibusters, heroes of a footnote in American history that just now has a special pertinence. The filibusters arrived at an exciting plan to resolve, simultaneously, the problems of countering foreign influence, finding new slave territories, and realizing the dream of gold and glory. The plan was simple enough: expeditions formed from the ranks of the discontented could be launched southward—Cuba, Mexico, Nicaragua, and Venezuela were popular targets—and once these territories were conquered, they could be opened to settlers from the slave states who would transform them into prosperous outposts of a new American empire, bulwark against any European expansionism.

In the dozen years between the Mexican and Civil wars, the filibusters enjoyed popular support and led thousands of soldiers of fortune, with musket and cannon, by ship and on horseback, to invade foreign lands. Under certain administrations—most notably those of Franklin Pierce and James Buchanan—the filibusters thrived, operating sometimes with what seemed tacit approval of the highest authorities. Officially, the United States respected Spain's dominion in Cuba and made formal efforts to purchase the island. Unofficially, members of the cabinet and Congress agreed that the colony was so vital to their interests that, if it could not be bought, it must eventually be taken by force of arms. They held a similar view of the northern provinces of Mexico.

The emotions, attitudes, and principles that fueled the filibusters' adventures have deep, strong roots in America. The word derives from the Spanish *filibustero,* a corruption of the Dutch *vrijbuiter,* that is, freebooter, pirate, buccaneer. But the English syllables have a rude jocularity, a raffish, heavy-booted spirit that accords with their happy suggestiveness—Fill 'em 'til they bust!—and the sinister rapacity of piracy is thus transformed into a big, brash, roll-up-the-sleeves and go-get-it opportunism, democratic and American. The word implied also a sweeping, grandiose gamble: a handful of daring men striking not merely for a galleon or two, but for an entire country. And underlying such high-stakes play, justifying the whole enterprise, was the assumption that Americans—the white race in its most vigorous and advanced incarnation—were destined to rule the hemisphere and so preserve it from the disorder and backwardness into which those of dark, inferior blood had allowed it to lapse.

The most famous of the filibusters was the one-time lawyer and hack journalist William Walker, who entered Nicaragua in 1855 with a tiny band of fifty-eight armed men from the California gold fields and made himself, a few months later, first the commander-in-chief and finally the president of the country. Walker had tried to conquer Mexico first, invading Baja with a somewhat larger force two years earlier, but found the few inhabitants of the region hostile to his practice of requisitioning their cattle and corn as provender for his liberating forces. When they could find no more ranches to pillage, the expeditionary army scampered over the border to avert reprisal.

In Central America his Falange enlisted on one side of a civil war, ostensibly as "colonists," but as the fortunes of war turned his way and several hundred additional disaffected miners and drifters arrived from the United States, Walker saw and seized the opportunity to make himself dictator. His exploits were celebrated briefly in major newspapers and in the halls of Congress, but Walker's hold on his new country was precarious and he made several serious errors. He alienated important families and former supporters by shooting the wrong people. He appointed gringos to the highest positions, made English legally equivalent to Spanish on all documents, and required new registration of all land titles. To his diary he confided that these measures were "to make the ownership of the lands of the State fall into the hands of those speaking English." Many Nicaraguans perceived the gist of his policies and invited the Costa Rican, Guatemalan, and Honduran armies to help oust the foreign invaders. Within six months Walker was at war on several fronts.

On the southern seaboard, especially in New Orleans, Walker's supporters held rallies, collected funds, and recruited soldiers to supply his "victorious" army, and he obliged them by legalizing slavery in his new nation. Here his choice was shrewd, for many wealthy merchants and shippers clung to the dream of a slave empire to be carved out of the Latin world. But the immediate value of Nicaragua, as Walker knew well enough, lay in its control of a transit corridor linking the Atlantic coast and the California gold fields. Before the Panama Canal and the transcontinental railroad, the quickest and cheapest route was by steamer to the Miskito Coast, thence up the San Juan River to Lake Nicaragua, from whose western end it was a mere eleven miles to the Pacific shore. By the time of Walker's conquest and occupation, nearly fifty thousand passengers a year were crossing the isthmus through Nicaragua, most of them on the steamers of Commodore Vanderbilt's Accessory Transit Company.

One of the new president's greatest errors was his canceling of Vanderbilt's franchise for this route in order to hand the lucrative trade over to two cronies. The Commodore was a ruthless and unflinching enemy where his financial interests were involved, and his agents, intriguing with the Costa Rican army, succeeded in seizing the transit corridor and thus depriving Walker of both revenues and reinforcements for his mercenary army. His forces cut in two, the new president saw his government collapse in a matter of weeks. Although as a farewell gesture the Americans blew up the three-hundred-year-old city of Grenada, a ship's captain managed to negotiate the escape of Walker and a battered remnant of his Falange.

Although he had spent hundreds of thousands of dollars and led most of his followers to their graves, victims of combat or cholera, Walker returned to a hero's welcome in New Orleans. It was enough for the zealots of filibusterism that he had *almost* succeeded. At once the indefatigable Walker launched fresh schemes to reconquer his adopted country. He found new partisans and backers; arms were purchased, recruits solicited, a ship chartered. This craft skulked through the Caribbean, ran aground on a reef, and had to be abandoned. In 1860 Walker and 110 men boarded another ship for a final assault. They held Trujillo for a few days before being surrounded by Honduran troops. A British commander arranged for the deportation of most of this miserable army but turned Walker over to the Hondurans, who promptly shot him.

It might seem obvious now that Walker's ambitions were absurd, his pose as the "protector" of the "barbarous" Indians a cruel and monstrous joke, his whole career a gothic aberration only possible in a time now forever past. You could see it all as a rare constellation: the putrefying delirium for gold joined with a dangerous popular myth (Manifest Destiny) under the sign of a demented but charismatic individual. But my father would not have seen it that way.

The Walker case, for Waldo, might undergo an ingenious bend or two and be bootlegged directly into the context of his tale about Grandfather and the old prospector, who by now has recovered enough to gesture and get out a word or two. In the butter light of the kerosene lamp—Grandpa would have

127

taken off the glass shade and wiped away the soot—it is possible to examine the foot, finally identified as the source of the powerful hint of decay in the cabin's stew of odors. Gangrene had set in, relieved only marginally by the old man's half-hearted attempt at amputation, and although the infection has since abated under its crust of scabs, it is now necessary to dress this second, older wound. One can visualize Granddad's disgust, how he wrinkles his nose as he begins unwrapping the limb from dirty bedding, how at last he begins to piece the story together. He sees that everything began with the toe—now phosphorescent blue-black, like the torso of a bottle fly—and a splinter, a blister, an untended bruise. The old man's averted eyes confirm the fact.

Everyone knows sore toes are sensitive. Except for toothache there is nothing like the instant, ice-pure agony of stubbing an already swollen toe. But everyone is likewise aware of the ignominy. A broken arm or rib seems noble by comparison, let alone the magnificence of a scar from bullet or shrapnel. We might cry out against the injustice: one man is blown flat, too stunned to feel anything, and comes home at the head of a parade, while another kicks idly at the cat and then with bulbous foot in the air, moaning like a dove, becomes an embarrassment to family and friends.

Ah, but suppose you were all alone! Had been alone for days, weeks, perhaps months! Had been driven to this isolation by the persistent canker of hope—delusion, the rest of the world might say—a belief however faint that some day soon the pick would pry into a seam of fabulous wealth, a salvation and absolution for the years of hardship and self-abnegation, a release from the dread suspicion that you have become a crank, a solitary, an anachronistic joke, a downright fool. To realize then that sheer, idiotic neglect—of a splinter, say, acquired by sallying forth in stockinged feet to split kindling on a cold morning—might bring you to a slow, shameful end; that you might actually die of—oh ridiculous, huge, purple-green, stinking!—of a . . . sore toe! Great God in Heaven—Jesus Christ on a crutch, Waldo would cry—such a realization could be too much to bear. A man might lunge after a more daring and dramatic fate, a final, desperate act of self-assertion.

It was out of sympathy for such a pathetic son-of-a-bitch that my father digressed—not at this point in the story but at any point, as fancy took him—onto the subject of Grandfather's own ultimately worthless claim and the machinations of the Bunker Hill and Sullivan Mining Company. For beneath Grandfather's irritation and disgust his son had detected a secret fellowship with the old prospector. After the Thunder Mountain boom Granddad too had toiled to find some trace of the dream, had in fact picked up good samples along the Deadwood. But already the day of the independent miner was passing. When the Hall brothers struck a good-sized lode directly across the river from the Baker claim, they sold out quickly and before long Bunker Hill arrived. They surveyed and sampled, staked out or purchased every valuable claim, then moved in compressed air drills, winches, ore cars, and a smelter. Granddad was first offered fifteen hundred dollars for title to his ground, but he held out for five thousand. Within a few months it was clear the vein ran in the opposite direction and his claim was worthless.

Partly for this reason and partly because this was the company that Bill Haywood and the Wobblies fought so bitterly in north Idaho, my father invoked Bunker Hill and Sullivan as a prime example of the inhuman rapacity of large corporations. It was an article of faith with him that the world was divided neatly between the great mass of wage-slaves, honest and hard-working people, and their exploiters, a handful of shadowy, bloated creatures who ran the juggernaut of high finance from their foul den on Wall Street. He held that a man on his own had no chance against these parasites. They named their own price, and you took what you could get (as Grandmother never tired of reminding Granddad he should have done). Their obscure manipulations of the market and contempt for those whom they exploited were mainly responsible for the human dilemma, for high prices, plane crashes, cancer, and bad teeth, even for the damned fool tricks people like the old prospector were driven to play on themselves. The connections were too complex and subtle to be entirely explicit, but Waldo felt them there, solid as the ground under his feet.

Then I suspected his eulogies of Soviet Russia and his torrents of invective against capitalism. They were too fierce to be true. They were also part of the context of almost all his tales and could be propelled to the forefront on a whim, posing again the danger that the original story might be submerged in white-hot fulminations against a distant enemy.

"The sonsabitches don't give a good goddamn about anything except profits."

"*Waldo*" (Mother).

"Start a war for the plain and simple goddamn reason there's another depression on the way."

"Why hell yes" (Uncle). "If a man makes a goddamn pair of shoes ever hour and they sell for ten dollars and he gits a dollar an hour there's your capital, by God, which has took possession of the means of perduction and also for damn sure the other nine dollars, which by God they lend back to the poor bastard and make inturst off it."

"That ain't but just the start of it. Purty soon everybody's got his pair of shoes. Then what the hell they goin' to do?" Here my father might lift the stove lid and spit into the firebox, listening momentarily to the sizzle as a kind of punctuation to the question.

"Munitions," my uncle would say after this dramatic pause, and Waldo would drop the lid back with a clang.

"Why shit yes, munitions. And Rockyfeller and the rest of them barons of high finance lend them little pissant dictators all the dollars they need to buy the pistoleros to keep the workers down for the goddamn banana company. The sonsabitches can't wait—"

"*Waldo!*"

But I often forsook the kitchen before my mother's final, despairing cry. There were no bears, no Indians, and no children in these rodomontades, and I could not understand the disparity between their abstruseness and their ardor. The Depression my parents worried over was incomprehensible to me—an empty, silly dread like a child's fear of the dark. Grown up, I learned that Waldo was evicted from a few logging camps for his agitating, his belief in the eight-hour day, and his objection to overcutting. I also came to see how his arguments—whacky, discontinuous, entirely warped by idiosyncratic personal experience—had the unerring accuracy of divinations. They required translation but always contained a bright sliver of truth. He would not have to be told that the formidable Cornelius Vanderbilt could employ the armies of foreign powers in the service of his profits or that Walker involved U.S. congressmen and respectable merchants in his schemes of conquest. He would grasp instantly how the gold rush was both context and prime mover of the whole tragicomic opera, for he knew that greed always determined foreign policy. He would be the first to trumpet the parallels between the filibusters and the Central Intelligence Agency, to explain to the unenlightened how perfectly consistent we were, for right now—this is the special pertinence of the Walker case—agents of the United States are fomenting a new invasion of Nicaragua, after the failure twenty years ago of an expedition to reconquer Cuba.

It's just the same, Waldo would say, the exact goddamn same. And it would be true that we are proceeding now again as "liberators" and "protectors" of the Miskito Indians, that we have in mind forming a new government, responsive to our interests, and that we accuse foreign usurpers, not the English now but the dread Russians, of infiltrating and manipulating the country for their own malign purposes. It may even be true as well that underlying this professed libertarian stance are the same old assumptions about the inability of those dark, degenerate runts to handle their own affairs, and about the necessity of enslaving them (though now it is the slavery of Coca-Cola and blue jeans and Hollywood), the same old assumptions about our ultimate and predestined dominance, our "sphere of influence" now expanding to encompass something called the "Free World," by which we mean possibly not only the whole world but remote caverns of space as well.

So Waldo would predict, and I think accurately, that the United States will invade Nicaragua (or some other pissant country) on the pretext of "liberating" its citizens, probably at the invitation of an exiled "freedom fighter," and that this invasion will be vigorously endorsed by the executives of many corporations (like Bunker Hill and Sullivan or American Smelting and Refin-

131

ing or the Homestake Mining Company) and that the soldiers who will die in the jungle are young men who yearn obscurely for a transcendent glory because life has not become the golden dream they expected, and finally that official propaganda will justify the invasion as a necessary defense against an evil and alien philosophy.

He might well go further, apprised of the dangerous indebtedness of Mexico, Brazil, Venezuela, Argentina, Bolivia, Peru. We are told these countries may default on huge loans given them by the largest American banks, bringing about serious financial crises in the Free World. The likelihood of such default increases, of course, if more countries follow Nicaragua in throwing out leaders sympathetic to the Free World and its banks. Waldo would be perfectly convinced that behind the fear of Russian malevolence lurks the same old greed of the big outfits, who simply want their profits or interest payments high and steady, and hence instruct the government to keep the little brown people tractable, deeply in debt, and anxious to purchase our newest gimcracks.

My father would, however, avoid a difficulty which I intend to face: the matter of connecting this complicated situation—more complicated than he knew, for he could never admit the ruthless, mind-numbing dogmatism of Marxism—to our lonely and barely alive prospector, and hence to the magic power of gold. Waldo did not often fool with this sort of connection. He preferred to let the stories chain together in their own pattern. But then, he never wrote anything down but lists of parts and supplies. It could be argued from my position that some thread is necessary, however fine, to stitch these matters to paper; and if we are dealing with the last century in the Americas, that thread will have a yellow glint.

Two months ago I boarded a train in Chihuahua for the eight-hour trip to Creel, a lumber town on the high, arid plateau that extends from northern Mexico into Canada. In Creel I planned to locate a guide for a journey on horseback into the Barranca del Cobre, a series of six gigantic fissures in the earth, more extensive and much less traveled than the Grand Canyon of the

Colorado. Three centuries ago the Tarahumara retreated deep into these canyons, where a remnant of the tribe still survives. They were fleeing the Spaniards who came looking for gold and silver beyond the great mines at El Oro, Parral, and Santa Eulalia.

Creel is near the Continental Divide, the tremendous upthrust of tectonic plates which brought precious metals to the surface, where erosion could carry them into watersheds throughout western North America, from the Yukon to the Rio Grande. The search for gold thus leads swiftly and inexorably from delta upstream into foothills and mountains, from coastal cities into desolate and savage highlands. After the big strikes, in an inverse progression, the lone prospector gives way to the mining gang, with common rockers and Long Toms, which are in turn supplanted by corporations with great mechanical earthmovers and crushers. The sourdough's isolated cabin is supplanted by a huddle of tents, then a row of false fronts, then a bustling city with sawmill, slaughterhouse, bank, hotel, theater, and mortuary.

I was deliberately trying to reverse these geographical and temporal patterns, proceeding by jet from San Francisco to the train from Chihuahua to the horses in Creel. I was traveling thus, backward through centuries, partly to recover from a long struggle over a billion and a half dollars' worth of gold. This gold, in the form of a fine powder scattered through the heart of a mountain, lies only five miles from my back door. The struggle was between me and ten of my neighbors, and the largest gold mining company in the United States. They wanted to dig up the mineral; we wanted it left in the ground.

The Homestake Mining Corporation proposed to dam a creek to make a reservoir, construct a slurry line from the crusher to the refiner, and blast a mile-long open pit from which they would take thirty-four thousand tons of ore a day, working twenty-four-hour shifts, for twenty-five years. The operation would occur in an area known as Blue Ridge, a spur of the Vaca Mountains in northern California. Blue Ridge is the highest point in our county, a haunt of the last bears, bobcats, and eagles in this region, and a major watershed for the river that irrigates farmland in our valley.

My neighbors and I wished to preserve this scrap of wild country, and we

133

feared pollution from the cyanide-refinement process and the mercury-bearing serpentine rock in which the gold was finely dispersed. There were other reasons, too, which are harder to articulate. They have to do with that mystical fascination of gold, with certain fanatic commitments of our civilization, and ultimately with a great paradox: the infinity of human desire in a fragile and finite world.

Trying to formulate these reasons we learned many things. For example, the situation on Blue Ridge is being duplicated in many places in the mountainous West. Long-abandoned mines are being reopened; ore deposits once passed over are being reassessed; geologists in helicopters are combing terrain forsaken by prospectors fifty years ago. All the easily worked gold deposits on the planet have long been known and most are exhausted. In South Africa, the world's biggest producer of gold, black men are now toiling two miles below the surface in shafts only forty inches high, where the temperature is a constant 130 degrees Fahrenheit. They must bring up three tons of ore to obtain for the owners a single ounce of gold. On Blue Ridge it will be six tons to an ounce.

Similarly the diligent Chinese had reworked the tailings from the forty-niners' sluice boxes, and then placer miners came with giant hydraulic hoses to blast away these tailings, the old sluice boxes, the shanties of the Chinese, and large chunks of the Sierra foothills. Fifty years ago they quit because the price of gold no longer justified such massive operations, and gradually a scant growth of shrubs and the tougher weeds crept over the craters and mounds of raw gravel. Now mining companies have returned with mightier machines, an improved technology. They are anxious to stake more millions on squeezing bullion from these thrice-mined heaps of debris.

All significant mineral extraction is now done by large corporations that employ dozens of lawyers, public relations experts, and advertising agencies as well as geologists and engineers. These corporations no longer face hostile Indians and a trackless, difficult terrain. Their enemies are small farmers and ranchers, rural communities, sportsmen, and environmentalists. These groups find themselves in the novel position of a new tribe of white aborigines, their "primitive" way of life threatened by a colossus, formidably organized and equipped. Their arguments, delivered before county planning commissions and boards of supervisors, sound oddly quaint and sentimental—appeals to the integrity of the land, respect for wild creatures, the priceless heritage of pure air and water.

To oppose this motley tribe, Homestake sent to the Yolo County courthouse a steady succession of pleasant, quiet-spoken company representatives and hired consultants. They wore expensive suits and carried briefcases full of charts or portable projectors with colorful slides. They were themselves, they said earnestly, environmentalists. The Homestake Company was committed to a safe, clean operation. They proposed a game refuge, a raptor-monitoring station, a program to transplant the endangered adobe lily. They argued that the new mine would be an overall improvement in the ecosystem. Areas previously vandalized by Suzukis and Yamahas or overgrazed by ravenous Herefords would be protected from such depredations.

The reservoir was described as "wildlife habitat improvement." Since the country is dry and hot in the summer, they presumed transient deer, coyotes, raccoons, or rabbits would be so grateful for these shimmering acres of water that they would overlook the tons of explosives being detonated a few yards away. Late in the county's deliberations someone noticed in passing that the project described a six-foot chain-link fence around the reservoir. Still later we learned about the security men and attack dogs patrolling the project area. Clearly those thirsty deer and raccoons would not be encouraged to tarry.

Miraculously, the county's government was able to peer over the chain-link fence and see an improved habitat. Similarly they could see beyond the apparent threat of an active seismic fault underlying the cyanide-rich tailings pond, and beyond the gross statistics for suspended particulates (dust) and heavy metals (poison). Ignoring petitions from thousands of county residents, they amended an ordinance which gave a tax advantage to land held for agricultural purposes. This amendment specifically allowed the impounding of water for mining operations on "agricultural" land, so that Homestake obtained both the reservoir and the tax break.

The articulate, well-dressed corporate team smiled with quiet assurance, packed up their slide shows and vanished, the bulldozers rumbling in on their heels. They had always been confident, and in fact they were unbeatable, because they had touched a deep, vital American nerve. That nerve is—in this case literally—golden opportunity. *Bonanza!* We could tell, even in the badinage at early public hearings, that officials were pleased and excited by the notion that gold had been "discovered" in their district. They had been used to reviewing building permits involving a few thousand dollars, and now there was talk of billions. *Billions in pure gold!*

It made little difference that no individual could pan a dime's worth of dust, because a giant corporation had purchased the mineral rights for fifty-two square miles of territory around the pit, and because the gold was so finely dispersed in the serpentine rock that only a massive earth-moving operation could recover it. The myth was that gold meant prosperity, somehow, for everyone. Bonanza was expressed in terms of jobs and tax revenues, and at the opportune moment the Homestake team spoke reverently of the "balance of payments." There was an implication that the health of our nation, the nourishment of every man, woman, and child, our collective defense against the forays of greedy foreigners—all these were crucially affected by this drive to smelt eighty tons of gold out of the mountain at our backs.

In the face of such awesome implications, what responsible official would side with a little band of fanatics prating of the rural way of life, of air and water cleaner than the legal requirements, of elk and eagles and Indian graves? We were fluff-headed idealists who didn't understand the hard economic realities, and one of the supervisors tried to set us straight. If there's gold up there on Blue Ridge, he said, then it's *got* to come out; everybody knew this—surely we did too—and Yolo County ought to get its cut of the cake.

So I fled from this oppressive truth—gold, billions in gold, *must* be dug up—fled to a dusty little Mexican town on the edge of a chasm where the last of the Tarahumara live. Mexico—one of those countries so deeply in debt, so troubled by economic problems, so unfortunate in its "balance of payments." But because of the interplay of currencies, my strong dollars against the inflated peso, I could buy a train ticket, take a room for two days at the Parador—the lone air-conditioned hotel with bar and restaurant where the girls wore starched white blouses and spoke broken English— and rent two horses for a week with less cash than I would pay at home for one night in the Sheraton.

It took a while to find the horses. The sardonic manager of the Parador gauged my Spanish good enough to allow direct negotiations with a Señor Gutierrez, if I could find him, who was the sole agent for such tourist transport. An old man, quite drunk but with a new hat and boots bracketing his soiled shirt and trousers, overheard us and volunteered to take me to Señor Gutierrez's very house. He knew the man and we could speak as friends. At dusk we crossed the railroad tracks and walked along unpaved streets, lined by adobe warrens where ragged and snot-nosed children observed us from dark doorways. Motor bikes and autos raised a gray, powdered stone that stung the eyes and grated between the teeth. The old man talked volubly of my prospects for a wonderful and scenic journey. He did not appear to notice the children or the dust.

In front of Señor Gutierrez's small house was a roofed cement patio where a single electric bulb burned over two wooden chairs, some loose boxes, and an eviscerated engine block, apparently removed from a pickup in the driveway. A person with a flashlight emerged from beneath the chassis, a squat and unsmiling man in grease-smudged tee shirt. My guide inquired politely if Señor Gutierrez the elder were available for consultation on a business matter, and the squat man disappeared inside.

Señor Gutierrez the elder emerged with his hat already on, listened to my companion's deferential introduction, and motioned us to advance to the little patio. He went back inside to get a third chair, and after we took our seats he carefully removed his hat and listened again while the old drunk explained the proposed wonderful journey into the Barranca, which was, of course, contingent upon the availability, or the possibility of the availability, of horses.

Señor Gutierrez considered this possibility. He was built like his son, with a large, solid belly, and the hands holding the hat were rough and capable. In the hard shadows of the electric light I could not read his face, beyond an impression of many knobs and ravines. There was no pasture for horses in the Barranca, he said. The canyon may be seen by jeep under the supervision of Señor Lalo at the Parador. Also it would take several days to ride there and back. The drunk also removed his hat and coughed. The gentleman has already foreseen the possibility of renting the animals for such a period of time, a truly extensive journey. Though of course a guide would be necessary. Therefore two horses at the minimum.

I can't take him, Señor Gutierrez said. He could go by jeep much more easily. Of course a guide, but who is there but the Indian boy? There are only two horses, at the maximum. Four days or five?

It depends, I said, But two horses is enough.

Your bed and food?

I have a special sleeping sack, very small, and I can provide my food. I have ridden on these journeys in North America and understand how it is.

There are no houses. You have to sleep out and take everything.

I understand that.

If you are longer than five days there will be a special charge for pasture.

That is agreeable.

Señor Gutierrez considered again for a time. Fifteen thousand pesos, he said.

Very good. (A few thousand one way or the other is nothing to the people of the strong dollar.)

There was a pause, broken only by the clink of a wrench from beneath the pickup.

Good, then. Señor Gutierrez shifted a little in his chair. Perhaps we would like a *sota*. He turned and called through the screen door to someone inside, and after a while a woman came out with three grand Coca-Colas.

As we drank the Coca-Colas Señor Gutierrez asked where I lived, how old I was, and whether I liked this part of Chihuahua. It was a hard country. Hot days and cold nights and the dust. In winter there was a meter of snow. But beautiful. The Barranca was something to see. A few people lived there too. The Indians and others. I would enjoy myself. There was nothing to worry about. The guide was a boy, but he knew his way. Did I have boots?

I had no boots, only these light shoes especially for sport.

For the first time, Señor Gutierrez manifested serious doubt. No boots? He shook his head. For such an extensive trip and horses one should have boots.

I assured him these sport shoes were adequate. Light and tough like the sandals worn by the Indians. There was no problem.

He shrugged. It was my decision. We finished the Coca-Colas, thanked him for his generosity, and rose to leave. I will call at the Parador at seven o'clock, Gutierrez the elder said. Be ready. You can go first to the market with the boy and get food.

Returning, the old drunk and I stopped at what appeared to be the liveliest bar in town. It had an interior of rough pine, hung with a few rusty tools and some moth-eaten coyote and lynx hides. The chief ornament, positioned on a counter, was a rotund pink and yellow ceramic pig with plastic flowers sprouting from its back. Most of the clientele were swaggering young urban *vaqueros* in wide hats, boots and jean jackets, gathered around an occasional young woman in tight pants and eyeshadow. At one booth sat four men, two of them in vestiges of a uniform, balancing automatic rifles on their laps. Middle-aged, big-bellied, they looked at everyone with a slow, arrogant regard.

The old man ignored the youths and the police, just as he overlooked the dust and the children. He informed me that there was no hard liquor but we could have at least a beer, to celebrate my bargain. I had made a very good arrangement, he said. Extraordinary. Fifteen thousand pesos was not so much, for two horses over five days. It would be something indeed wonderful to ride so far into the canyon. He saluted me as a gentleman.

139

I asked about the men with the rifles, and he gave a small, pursed smile and shook his head deprecatingly. There were occasionally bad people about, criminals. The police through their presence discouraged such people. Mexico was a place where many people were poor, and some were desperate and dishonest, so effective measures were necessary. But everything was going well now. Politics did not enter in. It was a matter of thwarting straightforward robbery and the marijuana trade.

I wanted to ask why politics did not enter in, but I knew that the old man would find such a discussion difficult in this context of friends and gentlemen celebrating the conclusion of a business arrangement. We finished our toast and separated rather ceremonially in the street outside. He mentioned that he would be on hand at seven in the morning to wish me a good journey. No matter the hour, he had nothing else to occupy him.

Walking back to the Parador, I thought about how politics must in fact have entered in somehow when I paid for the drinks: a few cents to me but a large and generous gesture for the old man. Not because of any superior talent or strength on my part, or ignorance or weakness on his, but merely because the balance of payments had arranged it so. It was this way for all the tourists at the Parador. They were mostly elderly, white-haired and florid and well fed for a lifetime, full of garrulous energy.

Just outside the plate glass of the restaurant windows passed the poor of Creel, Indian women bent under their baskets, barefoot and dirty children with eye infections, unshaven men reeling from doorway to doorway. They looked inside, but without expression, as people look at clouds. The tourists looked outside, too: swift glances as if what they beheld had the fascinating, unhealthy brightness of a welder's arc. But I did not see anything to explain the difference; it had to be a distant, political thing, like the balance of payments.

Gold has something to do with the balance of payments. I had learned that from Homestake. Countries that have gold reserves are more likely to maintain strong currencies. People have "confidence" in such countries. Even if something happens to the government—a revolution or war or scandal—there is still the gold. The United States has dollars, the strongest currency—the standard, in fact, against which all others are rated—and it also has more gold than any other country.

The United States is so powerful and reassuring that other countries and international agencies deposit their assets here. About 40 percent of all the gold ever mined—a stock of thirty-five thousand tons—is held in the vaults of large international banks, and our Federal Reserve in New York stores the largest single lode (around eleven thousand tons). The Bank of England and three Swiss banks have got most of the rest. This eleven thousand tons belongs actually to the central banks of seventy-three other countries or international institutions who are a bit uncertain of their own stability and feel more comfortable with bullion stashed in New York.

Of course the United States has its own private reserves of around eight thousand tons—the largest supply of any country and more than twice as much as the nearest competitor—so that all together we hold nearly two-thirds of all the "official" gold in the world. And we once had even more. At the end of World War II, after ten years of a government monopoly on the gold supply, the U.S. had stockpiled twenty-two thousand tons in Fort Knox, about one-half of all the gold mined since the time of the Pharaohs. The rich, traditionally, have made themselves strong in order to protect their riches, and in 1945 we were indisputably and overwhelmingly the greatest industrial and military machine the world had ever seen.

In this position of strength our money was "good as gold." Dollars were cherished everywhere in the world. A dollar was a piece of America, the biggest, safest, strongest place on earth—where the gold was, where the guns were—and to get dollars other countries sold us whatever they could or borrowed as much as they dared, and then came back with the dollars to buy the precious things we produced: autos, washing machines, jet fighters, movies. All other currencies were pegged to ours, and until 1968 ours was so solid we had only to guarantee that a quarter of its face value could be redeemed in gold. This was just a bit of insurance, a homage to that final principle of uncertainty: governments, even the greatest, may falter, and when they do investors lose confidence in signs and seals and symbols. Banknotes can become cigar lighters or mattress stuffing. Only the dense, pure, unchangeable metal endures.

Countries like Mexico have at most a few dozen tons of gold reserves. All the nations of Latin America taken together own less than one-tenth of the U.S. holdings. There is a double irony here: once the Aztecs possessed great stores of gold, almost all of it stolen by the Spaniards, who with this booty made themselves briefly splendid. Time has, however, struck its own balance of payments. It has been argued that this brutal theft brought a proper revenge, that the sudden influx of Aztec and Incan treasure ultimately ruined Spain, encouraging meaningless extravagance and unwise further expeditions, at the expense of developing dependable domestic industries.

Mexico in any case can hardly gloat. The old mines produce very little. The peso is turning worthless at a brisk rate. Mexico has borrowed heavily, so paying interest on its debt (in dollars) is an ever-increasing burden. The great banks grow skittish, demand harsh terms for any further loans, which Mexico must have to pursue its schemes of progress. Harsher loans, higher interest, weaker currency will likely doom these schemes, frightening banks even more, so they demand still sterner conditions, and so forth, and on and on and on. A greater and greater imbalance: North Americans growing ever larger, ruddier, more boisterous; the Mexicans forever diminishing, gaunt and hungry and sullen under their Sisyphean debt.

But they were all there in the morning, hale and cheerful: Señor Gutierrez, Señor Lalo, and the old man, now sober and even more deferential. Everyone saluted everyone else. I displayed my pack containing the special sleeping sack, and received admonishments and benedictions for this wonderful and significant journey, now beginning. A tour bus was also loading at the door. The old folks, dressed brightly and equipped with cameras and shopping bags, chattered as we detoured around them. They would be stopping at an Indian village, I gathered, to buy native things, and would still have time to overlook the canyon and return to the hotel for dinner. If you buy postcards that picture the Tarahumaras, I heard the guide say, you must enclose them in an envelope, or the government will not allow them through the mail, since it is believed they do not fairly represent the progress of Mexico.

The *caballos* were already saddled and tied to the bumper of the immobile pickup by the time we rounded the corner. They resembled mutant jackrabbits, short-bodied and large of head, dwarfed by the monstrous saddles with their great, globular wooden horns. My sport shoes dragged in the dust. I looked at Señor Gutierrez, stricken by suspicion, but he was already rummaging about the patio, picking out two bridles. The guide was there, a slight boy who looked down and away after tugging on the brim of his tractor cap. He too, I noticed, wore sport shoes.

This is Manuel, said Señor Gutierrez. You go to the store with him and get some food, while I fix this fucked bridle, and then everything is ready.

These are very small horses, I said.

Señor Gutierrez turned to regard me. Good horses, he said.

Very small.

Good horses, you will see.

One of the good horses farted. Manuel grinned, revealing huge, white teeth.

At the market I bought cans of frijoles and tuna, rice, flour tortillas, onions, limes and piquant sauce. Manuel bought a loaf of Bimbo bread and a chunk of baloney. He admitted to being seventeen and to living in Creel, but to all other inquiries regarding time, distance, or meaning he replied *¿Quien sabe?* grinning with eyes shut.

When we returned the horses were ready, dozing now at the bumper. Our provisions were stuffed in plastic shopping bags and hung from the great wooden horns. Señor Gutierrez had tied my pack to the cantle of the saddle on the largest of the jackrabbits, a dirty white gelding. Then there was a brief altercation over payment. I had brought the full fifteen thousand, but after seeing the horses I determined to pay only half at the outset. I lacked confidence in their ability to haul my eighty kilograms over the mountains for

143

four days. Señor Gutierrez reminded me that if we were out longer I would have to pay for extra pasture. A little sack of corn tied on Manuel's saddle was all the feed we had, just enough—he said—for four days.

You will see they are good horses. He laughed and I saw that he had no front teeth. But don't take them down to the canyon floor. You are not ready for that. He looked severely at Manuel. Do you hear? Manuel looked down and away, presumably a nod. All right. So long, *caballeros*.

We make our way out of town, past the sawmill with its mountains of peeled logs, on a gravel road that bends and dips over the rolling plateau. In early May the sun already has some authority: the sparse grass has yellowed and the scattered ponderosa, oak, juniper, and madrone are a dull and dusty green. The only brightness comes from the dark blood of manzanita bark and a rare scatter of paintbrush or a tiny yellow flower, possibly a variety of cinquefoil. From ridgetop, I see distant blue mountains or mighty rotten cores of igneous intrusion. Occasionally the trail winds near an outcropping, fractured basalt with a few streaks of dirty quartz, but I see nothing like the rich hues of the canyonlands of North America.

I feel ridiculous enough astride this surly white pony. My feet in the stirrups barely clear the ground, and my bulk atop the heavy saddle of leather and wood must appear to be moving by itself, decorated by a bowsprit of horsehead and a rudder of long hair. Still, after an hour of recalcitrance which Manuel overcomes with a rope-end, the horses plod up and down hill without sign of fatigue. We break away from the road and follow shortcuts, where Manuel without warning or apparent purpose flogs his mount into a dead run.

I have given up asking him why he does anything, or where we are, or what a certain plant or bird is called, for his answer is always the shrug, mute grin, *¿Quien sabe?* Several times he lies back in his saddle until his head rides on the horse's rump, grinning at me upside-down, and now and then he kicks out of his stirrups and jumps up to squat on his heels in the saddle, like a monkey. He does, however, know where he is. We branch off on a trail that passes by some boulders where he shows me a few faint

144

petroglyphs: circles, snake wriggles, and stick figures. *Quien sabe* what they mean. The Indians did it long ago. He agrees that he is half Tarahumara, from his mother. But he claims he doesn't know the language and doesn't have any idea who his father was.

We push on into the heat of afternoon, and a pattern is established. Manuel gallops ahead to find a shade tree on a ridge where there may be a little breeze; there he dozes until I catch up. Inevitably, we lose each other and I have to backtrack to find the point where he diverged onto another trail. I curse his lack of responsibility, dismounting often to search for his sign, and eventually strike the main road, where I encounter him again.

He is excited because he has just killed a rattler, so we double back a short distance to view the corpse, still writhing at the base of a pine tree. It is of moderate size, perhaps three feet, and the color of dust and shadow. A bit later in the afternoon we scare a lynx across the path, and the cat wears nearly this same camouflage. Here everything seems smaller, lighter, and duller than corresponding varieties in my homeland, as if disguising itself as dry stone or dead leaf, while the landscape is far vaster, more desolate, more alien in its barren uniformity than the northern ranges of the Divide. There is very little water, and not much life. Besides the snake and lynx I notice only the small, dun lizards that tickle through the dry leaves, the vultures that hang and slide in the sky, and an occasional group of skeletal cows. Rarely we pass a ribbon of water and a group of log huts, a little ploughed field littered with dead cornstalks, a few children and dogs playing in the dust.

In midafternoon we pull into a small settlement gathered around a mill— heaps of logs, a long shed over stacks of rough-cut lumber, and an old-fashioned five-foot circular saw. There is what is described as a store, a building clearly made like all the others out of the crude boards from the mill. A man and his wife stand behind the counter with their stock: several cases of Coke and Esprit, cans of motor oil, some tuna, beans, soap, and toilet paper. At the doorway two Tarahumara women sit with their children, pointedly ignoring us. After some talk and slight jokes we purchase six sotas,

145

drinking two and packing away the others, then mount up again. Only a kilometer or less from this village, Manuel says, we must camp on a creek, for it is the last water for a while.

We pick up the creek and follow the trail on its bank until we reach a smoke-blackened cave in a low rock bluff. Manuel tells me to unpack my pony and tie him to a certain tree. He must, he says, go in search of fodder, for we will be sleeping here in this cave. I know enough now not to ask him when he will return or if I should build a fire or whether to save him a burrito, but merely turn to undo my cinch as he gallops off like the Pony Express.

I collect some dry manzanita and juniper and start a small blaze, open a can of beans, and slice up an onion. While the beans warm in the pot I sit on a rock at the mouth of the cave and smoke a cigarette. In the last light I see a coyote move out of the brush along the creek and cross the trail. He pauses to watch me for a time before disappearing at a trot into the trees on the slope. He, too, is the color of earth and darkness. A few minutes later I hear a soft, regular sound, a light patting, and I guess what it is even before the man comes into view. A Tarahumara is running on the trail, his sandals with rubber tire soles flapping in the heavy dust. He waves and calls to me without breaking his perfectly regular pace, volunteering that he is going directly on into town and will see me again on his return. Then he disappears around a bend in the trail and the pit-pat diminishes and dies.

I spread out a few tortillas which I cover with the hot beans and onion and a dash of sauce, then roll them up tight in a pan placed by the coals. It is dusk when I hear the sandals flapping and the Tarahumara sails by again. He travels at the exact, same pace, but this time he swings in one hand a battered aluminum attaché case. He moves well inside his baggy trousers and old plaid shirt, not a jogging but a rapid forward glide, knees scarcely lifting, elbows hiking to reach rather than flail. Another smile and halloo and he is gone.

I am tired of waiting for Manuel, so I open a Coca-Cola and eat all but two of the burritos. I spread my sleeping bag outside the cave, so I can rest my sore tail-bone and see the stars. They are out, and a quarter-moon as well, by the time my guide returns with a great bundle of cornstalks athwart his pommel. The two ponies devour them noisily in the dark while Manuel gets his Esprit from the creek and, by firelight, falls on his Bimbo and baloney. He also dispatches the burritos, then makes his bed from the two horse blankets, using the saddle as a pillow. He accepts my offer of a cigarette, and in a rare burst of volubility tells me that we will ride out at dawn and reach the canyon easily by afternoon. The day after I can walk down to the river, where is it like another country, with oranges and lemons and all kinds of fruit. He will wait with the horses at the rimrock, where the only problem is the lack of pasture. Having divulged so much, he looks away, grins, and pulls the blanket up over his ears. Oranges and lemons? *Quien sabe.*

Breakfast is cold beans in tortillas and the last of the sotas, after which we feed the ponies a hatful of corn and move out just as the sun clears the treetops. The pattern is the same: Manuel undertakes inexplicable dashes, the ponies laboring uphill, and then dawdles along half-asleep. The terrain is steeper, more rock breaking through the earth's skin. We intercept roads only a time or two and do not follow them for long. Just after midday we reach benchlands riven by considerable canyons, and I begin to see in their rock walls some of the shapes described by the French poet and drug addict Antonin Artaud, who rode through here fifty years ago. It is indeed peculiar how many stones seem to have cracked and weathered to resemble living forms: eagles, apes, elephants, serpents, human figures huddled in a shroud or naked and full-bodied under the sun.

The silence all around—I hear only the clink of horseshoe or creaking of saddle leather—and the immense size of the sculpted forms produces an eerie feeling that we are being watched, brooded over, judged. Even Manuel is sobered, at least until we wind out of one of these canyons and discover ourselves on a flat, long field overgrown with manzanita and greasewood. Here is the airfield, he says happily.

I have learned not to ask direct questions. Military, I assert, and Manuel nods.

It does not appear much used.

Only two years ago.

Hunting guerrillas—politics.

No, *bandidos*—the marijuana.

Many soldiers.

Oh yes, many. Hundreds.

Can this be true? Large troop carriers landing in this desolate place, commandos fanning out into the bush, automatic weapons, firefights? Except for a wooden cross stuck in a heap of rocks, a trailside grave, we have not seen a sign of human occupation in some hours. There is no contrail in the sky, no smoke on the horizon, no flash from a distant tin roof. Only the two of us crawling like ants through the immense landscape, watched by silent stones. But then marijuana—remember Acapulco gold?—is one of the few commodities that assist Mexico in its effort to achieve the balance of payments. Perhaps the desperate will hide even here if the stakes are high enough.

Less than an hour later we reach the canyon rim and a scatter of abandoned buildings, their roofs and many walls destroyed, the collapsed floors strewn with rubble. I am amazed at the size of this ruin, for most of the buildings were of native rock, with connecting concrete walkways and patios. Some of the structures had several rooms, much larger than anything I have seen so far, aside from the sawmill shed. Manuel claims this was headquarters for the army until the bandidos were driven away, and then afterwards the Indians destroyed everything. Nearby, he says, there is still a mission school and at least one little hacienda. There he must ask about pasture and water.

But first we must find a camp, and that is an opportunity to take a look into the Barranca. When we reach its rim I see that it is indeed vast, but so different from our own Grand Canyon that I cannot compare them. The dark rock cliffs plunge downward, tier upon tier, with here and there a lone, eroded spire like a sentinel. There are a few bands or streaks of paler stone, one with a blue-green tint, but no flamboyant reds or yellows. The gorge, so deep I cannot see the river at the bottom, stretches from horizon to horizon, intersecting other canyons that appear, at least from a distance, to be equally vast.

On the opposite wall of this chasm there are crevices choked with bright green brush, giving me hope that we will have fresh water, but Manuel says the only spring nearby is at the hacienda, which belongs to a certain Perfeto. We unload our gear under the big pine at the very brink of the canyon, leaving the saddles on so we can ride back to the spring. Fortunately I have kept two of the Coca-Cola bottles, twelve-ouncers of heavy glass, and equipped them with stoppers carved from short sections of pine branch.

At the main hut of the hacienda three Tarahumara women sit with their children in the shade of an apple tree. They make no move to rise, and after long pauses give Manuel to understand that Señor Perfeto is not to be found, nor is any fodder available. Perhaps at the mission. We confer briefly, then my companion gallops off to verify this rumor and I am commissioned to fetch water.

I tie up the horse, take my Coca-Cola bottles, and follow two of the children down the mountain. We descend a flight of steps cut into rock to reach a little crevice where stands a pool perhaps three feet across. The water is opaque green below a film of dead insects, leaves, and clots of algae. I hear a commotion, a grunt, and in a moment the snout and forequarters of a pig emerge from a rock shelf just below the pool.

I turn to the boys, incredulous. One drinks this? They nod enthusiastically. I challenge them to prove it and the elder bends without hesitation and scoops up a mouthful. There seems to be no choice. I fill the bottles with the tepid stuff, hoping that a good boil and several drops of iodine will annihilate whatever creatures live in it. This is the only water, one boy volunteers, except for a pool by the old buildings which is only good for cows. You have cows, I say, but you have no feed for them. The boys look at each other. And Señor Perfeto is far away. They look at each other again, and nod solemnly. So it is.

I return to the camp under the tree and make a small fire to boil our twenty-four ounces of water. Manuel returns to report he has found no fodder but there is an old corral nearby where we can keep the horses. It is certain now we can stay no more than one day here. Early tomorrow I will have to proceed on foot into the canyon and climb out again in the afternoon. Having outlined the foreseeable future, Manuel goes off to tend to our mounts. I stroll along the canyon rim, wander through the ruined buildings, sit on a rocky point to watch the sunset.

The view is best to the east, where late, golden light spreads over the plateau to far blue mountains. At my feet the great cavern in the earth is filling with shadow. The tones of ochre and ash on the rock walls deepen into violet, amber, and indigo. Where the cliffs fall sheer to the invisible river it is already evening, except where a notch in the horizon allows a great shaft of rose light to strike through. A wind is driving now out of the north and west, and it is suddenly chill. I feel the ghost of that meter of snow recollected by Gutierrez the elder.

It is time to return to camp, don a sweater, and stir up the fire. We will have tuna and rice, doubtless with a medicinal flavor, then a cigarette, a little talk, and finally deep sleep under the sighing pine. And that is exactly how it is, but for a few moments near morning when I wake to see a partial moon over the horizon, like a halberd blade glowing red from the forge. The wind is gone and there is nothing in the immense and final stillness but the faint chink of a single bird.

Perhaps only silence and the phosphorescent stars have awakened me. Where I live in California is supposed to be rural, "the country," but one hears always a distant plane boring through heaven or a farmer's tractor discing a field across the road. Always at night there is an ambient glow from Sacramento and the recurrent rumble of trucks—I never know this utter emptiness and intense, perfectly silent celestial blaze. Even from the top of Blue Ridge, when I have climbed it, one can see a string of tiny, winking diamonds on the valley floor—the headlights of trucks moving on Interstate 5. And when I return the heavy tractors will be growling over Blue Ridge, hauling sand and gravel to build the Homestake dam, and after that the massive detonations will begin, the crushing of tons of rock for every precious ounce of gold.

150

All at once I know a desolation and hopelessness beyond anything I felt in the heat of the battle against the great strip mine. In the courthouse chambers, side by side with local farmers, I was filled with righteous fury and a bittersweet despair; we were right, after all—on the side of the deer and butterflies and all things wild and free—so there would be honor even in defeat. Our enemy was the giant, sinister corporation, those who would tear the heart out of a mountain in their fit of greed. I knew they were selfish and treacherous—I had my dead father's word, his loony Wobbly rage, to guide me. Once again it was the common people, the little people, against the fat cats with their secret money-game machinations.

But I was not seeing far enough then. Here, in this profound solitude, camped in an empty ruin and surrounded by a land so dry and broken and bare that everything alive shrinks and takes on the color of death, where only the colossal stones concentrate in themselves a power of articulate spirit—here I think I do see. I see to the south, under the hot blade of the moon, the Spaniards marching behind a cross, the heads of Indians on their pikes. They are searching for El Dorado, for the Seven Cities of Cibola, for another fabled land where men eat from plates of gold. It will take them a hundred years, but they will reach the banks of the Sacramento, see Blue Ridge, fire their muskets to cow the Wintun, who have pursued them mostly out of curiosity. For these last, rag-tag conquerors, the dream of gold will have evaporated—a tremendous irony, for they are only a few miles from the California Mother Lode. But they have become cynics, covetous mostly of land grants and slaves, already on the brink of a bloody revolution.

To the north I see the greater brigands, English speakers, the ultimate filibusters, who in the next century become the largest and most powerful nation on earth, controlling at last that gold hoard of which the Europeans dreamed, an unimaginable wealth which inspires confidence and fear everywhere, and to defend which new legions are sent forth in mighty metal dragonflies to hunt unbelievers and recalcitrants out of the jungles. But these modern warriors do not ride out in bright helmet and cuirass, with a shout for God and king. They are camouflaged like venomous lizards, bear

no identification, and cross borders to kill in secrecy. They carry—in case they find themselves trapped in an alien land—a little gold to barter for their lives.

Rummaging in the library for knowledge of such things, I have run across a fine and clear connection between our wealth and our power, between money and murder: a fact I could never cite to the county supervisors because it was a truth so bizarre. I need to resurrect Waldo for that job. Dad, I would have to say, things look bad. These shithouse mice are slicker than ever; it looks like the working people are going to take it again. But I've dug up something we can throw at them. Then I'd send him up the aisle at the courthouse toward the little witness lectern, stomping his gimpy leg (crushed by the hydraulic carriage of a logging truck), the fire of the Industrial Worker in his eye and backwoods sulphur on his tongue, to say the plain things that have to be said, that old men are still sending soldiers out to protect profits, that miser's gold is still bought with patriot's blood.

Remember that until 1968 the United States partially redeemed its currency at a rate of thirty-five dollars an ounce, yet so awe-inspiring was our position in the world that other nations actually preferred our dollars even to the excrement of the gods, as the Aztecs called gold. The offer of redemption was really only symbolic; nobody would turn in their sound dollars for gold, for that would mean they no longer trusted those dollars, which would mean they doubted the power of the United States to prevail against all comers, to impose its will, to be the biggest and the toughest and the richest of all, as we had been unflaggingly for twenty-five years, which would mean only gold counted again, the raw bullion itself, and not some twaddle about American "strength" or "resolve" or "destiny." Nobody could imagine such a dramatic loss of confidence. Nobody, that is, until the second week of March 1968, and then all at once everybody could imagine it.

In that one week the world's financiers, treasurers, and speculators bought back a thousand tons of American gold, more than ten percent of our reserves. Air Force jets flew night and day with loads of ingots to the Bank of England, piling up so many that the floor of the weighing room collapsed.

The Air Force also flew a lot of extra missions from Saigon to the West Coast that week, but the cargoes were stacks of plastic bags containing human corpses. For this was the aftermath of the Tet Offensive, a first unequivocal sign that the tide of battle had shifted and a tiny, indigent, war-ravaged nation inhabited largely by illiterate farmers and herdsmen was actually going to defeat a technologically advanced "superpower." This miracle brought about the furious commerce: we had to take in the dead soldiers at one end of the country and ship out the dead bars of gold at the other, until it was clear that we would run out of gold long before we ran out of infantry-men, and so we stopped—not the war, but the redemption of our money in precious metal.

The dollar, as the books delicately explain it, went into decline. The price of gold, on the other hand, went crazy, eventually rising to better than eight hundred dollars an ounce. A new, fast, hot game was organized at Comex, and so many players bought in that there was a shortage of chips. The miners dusted off their old maps and assay reports, and somewhere on a corporate desk the pointer paused, twitched, and finally struck down on Blue Ridge in Yolo County. The men around the table looked at one another, smiled, and rolled up their sleeves. This one.

And the thing I see now, the cause of this deep and final hopelessness—almost a peace—is that gold compels men's respect not because it is bright and durable and rare, but precisely because it bears with it the thrill of death. It redeems our mortality, reminds us that paper lies, friends fail, empires collapse. We believe, or pretend to believe, in the falsehood of its "security," but as mere bullion, mere "reserve," guarantor of transactions, it is forgotten, dead as a stone, an empty entry on the balance sheet.

In time of war and unrest, when the stench of cadavers is in the streets, gold begins to give off its true dark radiance; it grows antic and assumes many shapes—wafers, pigeon eggs, gossamer sheets, auto grills, suppositories—and travels across borders at night, or slips aboard fishing boats or unmarked planes to flee a continent. In the final collapse of the South Vietnamese government and Lon Nol's regime in Cambodia, the departing leaders tried frantically to arrange the transport of sixteen tons of bullion to banks in Switzerland. The United States arranged for a cargo plane, but in the confusion of the last days the transfer failed. Wealthy citizens escaping into Laos, however, brought gold hidden in a hundred ways—and found U.S. and European bullion dealers ready to buy. Alongside the kitchens and hospitals of the refugee camps were the booths of the gold traders, equipped with scales, testing equipment, and suitcases full of currency. In five months, fifteen million dollars changed hands.

It was the same in World War II, when Hitler's army chased the gold hoards of the French, Poles, and Norwegians, who dodged away on skis, in small boats, in truck convoys and merchant ships, bearing tons of ingots liberated at last from their vaults to draw men, like a great magnet, into fierce and bloody conflict. It has always been so. The dictator's last decision is a fine balancing of his desire to live and his love of gold. How much can be carried, at what risk? Who can he trust? What must he promise his guard? Where can the treasure be hidden again? A favorite place, we have noted, is the Federal Reserve in New York. There it is protected by nuclear submarines, strategic bombers, great missiles in their silos, a mighty umbrella of death that can cover the entire planet. An umbrella with a handle of gold.

In the morning I leave Manuel to guard our gear—he has dropped more allusions to the bandidos—and set off for the heart of the Barranca. Besides my camera, I take only a leftover burrito, a handful of candied peanuts and two limes. A thin enough ration, if Manuel is correct in warning me that although one may descend in an hour, the return takes at least three times as long. For the first half mile I merely follow an abandoned road along the rim, but then in a saddle between two low bluffs the road pitches down sharply into the canyon proper, becomes a trail, and soon the trail is a mere goat path, switchback after switchback cut into an almost sheer cliff face. Although the morning was cool enough, the sun soon clears the edge of the chasm and lays a lash across the nape of my neck. In less than thirty minutes the vegetation has altered dramatically: frantic chains of prickly pear erupt

155

through the thinning scrub oak, and I pass a variety of yucca that sends aloft a long spear of tightly packed golden flowers. The mesquite, now shrunken and skeletal, grows directly from the riven rock. I have brought no water, and the arid heat turns my sweat to a film of grit and salt. I cut and suck one of the limes. I worry no more about how many hours it will take me to hoist myself out of this hole, whose proportions grow more astounding with each switchback. I think only of the water below, the water that must be there.

After forty-five minutes it does appear, a necklace of deep green pools another two thousand feet below. Between the pools there is a white tumult over and around great boulders, and I can hear a faint, continuous rushing. That sound, coming through the still, hot air, tantalizes me out of all thought, and for some time I concentrate on the turn and drop of the trail, see only the puffs of dust and skittering pebbles under my own hurrying feet. Once, with a start, I see fresh horse or burro dung on the trail and look up. There is a man standing on a tiny terrace perhaps a quarter of a mile away, across an impassable cleft in the canyon wall. I wave slowly and deliberately, but he does not respond. When I look again he is gone.

I scramble the last few yards to the canyon floor, so hot, thirsty and exhausted that I pause only to sling my camera and lunch sack on the bank, strip to my shorts, and plunge into one of the pools, over my head in deliciously cold water. Water! A vast, slow deluge in which I roll and drink and blow like a porpoise. Floating on my back I see the columns of stone looming over me, rearing to the clouds. The faces and beaks of ancient gods are still there, but less formidable now, fringed by greenery, their own images shimmering at their feet.

When I have reveled enough in this exhilarating coolness, I heave myself onto a great flat rock and welcome the very sun that before seemed to be flaying me alive. So it goes for perhaps an hour, in and out, until finally I drift into a doze, mindless and idle under the spell of the river purring over the boulders. Traveling a single mile straight down into this tremendous fissure in ancient stone, I seem to have recovered the first birth, become old Adam, a creature of sun, rock, and water, without purpose or even will, luxuriating in the simplest and most powerful of sensations—that of pure being. This, surely, is what I came for.

There is a slight movement on the bank. I sit up with a start and see a man standing on a boulder across the river. He lifts one hand, his lips moving. I cannot hear over the rush of water, so he approaches, picking his way over the smooth rocks. He is wearing a plastic hardhat, and something dangles at the belt that holds up his khaki trousers. When he arrives he gives me a strong handshake, smiles warmly, and poses the usual questions. I see now that the object swinging from his belt is a carbide headlamp, the sure mark of the underground miner.

After I have explained how I came here, that I am only visiting, wandering, in search of nothing in particular, he offers me a Faro cigarette, the cheapest and crudest tobacco available, and tells me he is on his way back to his mine after lunch. He is called Anicleto, and he lives downriver a few hundred meters with his family, has lived there his whole life. If I would like to see the mine and the work and his home, he would be pleased to show me. After my bath I can follow the trail and find the opening to the shaft.

I ask what it is he mines, and whether others are at the same task. Gold, a little gold, is all they have. He and three or four others, his neighbors, are working now. The mines are very old. Since the time of the Spaniards. But the Tarahumaras never bothered. They moved into caves in the canyons only to escape the winters. We agree that they chose a remarkable place, and that indeed so many stones bear an uncanny resemblance to living things. Also the shift in climate is marvelous, for he confirms the existence of oranges and lemons. There is little gold left, but it is a good enough life.

He appears to be blessed with good health and genial spirits, a sturdy man with a plain, broad smile, clearly glad for my unexpected company. When we crush out our smokes and he rises to go, I thank him for his invitation and promise to visit the mine as soon as I am dressed and finished with my little lunch.

The trail—indicated by a casual wave—is not so clear, however, and I find myself again plodding in the heat along a network of narrow and twisting

tracks, often faint and overgrown with thorny brush. I pass another abandoned building, half in ruin. Then, rounding a shoulder of rock, I see coming
toward me a young man riding a burro. He hails me, immediately merry and
alert. What a surprise! He hops off the packsaddle, an old-fashioned
sawbuck draped with a burlap sack, and pumps my hand. Where am I going?
To which mine? He hitches his ragged trousers, held up by a bit of rope, and
grins in delight. He will take me to one he works with his father.

We soon sort out that he is Anicleto the Younger, the next oldest son, and
that I have missed the turnoff to their mine and so might have wandered for
hours through the canyon, except for this most fortuitous encounter. He
drives the burro ahead of us with a dead branch picked from the trail, and
before long we scramble up to a narrow ledge at what I take to be the
entrance to the mine. It is a hole in the mountain, no more than four feet
across, out of which blows a current of cool air.

Young Anicleto plies me with questions and information. What am I doing
here? Am I a tourist? To have come by horseback—this is highly unusual.
Only rarely does someone like myself appear, in any case. California—it
must be indeed wonderful. His father was once in Los Angeles and someday
he too would like to go and see for himself. As we converse he reaches
behind a rock and produces another headlamp, a jar of water and a little sack
of carbide. After loading the lamp with water and fuel, he pushes the plunger
to mix them and lights the jet of gas with a wooden match.

Taking the burlap sack in one hand, he waves the lamp in the other. Now
we go in. I should follow the light as he directs it back in my path, being
careful of the narrow places. It is not far and there is no reason to be worried. *Vamos!* And he is gone like a gopher into the dark, cool hole.

I crawl behind him, the light jogging and flickering on the damp, jagged
stone. Soon the tunnel constricts even more, and on hands and knees I must
squeeze through irregular passages, now up, now down, sometimes angling
to the side. The current of cold air is steady on my face, and I hear Anicleto
scuffling ahead of me, talking and chuckling occasionally to himself, but when
the light vanishes briefly at a bend, leaving an impenetrable darkness, I am

suddenly aware of the colossal tiers of rock poised a few inches above my back. I fumble along the rough wall, a strange, primeval panic stirring in my chest. An earthquake, the slightest of tremors, could grind shut this pitiful burrow. Perhaps even a dislodged stone, a shock of knee on the floor, the vibration of my rasping breath. I move as fast as I dare, banging head and shoulders on projecting rocks, suppressing a whimper, and then the tunnel mercifully widens, opens, becomes a cave in which now there are two lights and I can hear the ring of steel.

I make out that Anicleto Senior is perched on a crude ladder made of sections of sapling, working with hammer and cold chisel on the cave roof. At the foot of the ladder is a heap of broken rock, fist-sized pieces and smaller, which Anicleto Junior begins to stuff in his sack. His father flicks on a flashlight and shows me the vein he is following, a blue-green streak perhaps four inches wide, running from floor to ceiling. The copper makes the color, he tells me, but the gold occurs with it, too fine to see. He has nearly finished his sackload for the afternoon, so we can go on to the *taunas* and see how the rock is prepared for the mercury.

I wait for a few moments while the chisel works, slow clang after slow clang, and the last chunks of ore rattle to the cave floor. Anicleto Junior nips them up and stows them away, and when his father has descended from the ladder we all return through the tunnel. The trip out seems shorter by half, even though the young man must drag the heavy sack behind him. Outside, after slapping dust from our pants, we gather around one of the pieces of ore to examine it. A dull shade of turquoise, malachite probably, with no visible glints of riches. It is not much, the father says, shaking his head. Two or three sacks may bring a half gram or less—it comes to three or four of your yankee dollars a day. And the milling and retorting is yet to be done.

Anicleto Junior has thrown the sack on the burro, and we move off on the trail, downward toward the river. During the sharp descent we cross a rusted section of iron pipe two feet across and another considerable chunk of cast metal, now twisted and discolored, some bone of an industrial dinosaur. From the mining many years ago, Anicleto Senior tells me. Great machines they had then, brought down piece by piece with cables. The miners, I ask, lived in those ruins above, on the canyon rim? Quite so, he says. But when they left the Tarahumaras destroyed the roofs and caved in the walls.

As we approach the river the rusted iron pipe emerges again, but now it is humming and jets of mist blow from pinholes at the seams. At the bank the pipe terminates, spewing a powerful column of clear water toward a series of feeder conduits made from small logs cut lengthwise in half and scooped out. Two of these rude ducts are sluicing the water into strange contraptions that clank and grind amid the great boulders at the edge of the river. Two men lounge in the shade of a tree overhanging the bank, supervising the operation. Anicleto introduces me, seemingly pleased to provide a bit of diversion, while his son swings another duct into the jet of water. The miners explain to me proudly how they build these *taunas* and how they work.

A frame of heavy logs is built over a large, flat rock, in the middle of which another log is anchored vertically. Around this center post they place a cylindrical iron hoop, or tank without bottom or top, perhaps four feet in diameter. The hoop is sealed to the rock at the bottom so it will hold water. A crossbar at the top of the centerpost extends past the hoop and from it hangs a horizontal, encircling water wheel. The centerpost is held loosely to the log frame at the top and to the rock at the bottom, so that when a jet of water is directed into the wheel, it creaks into motion, rotating the post inside the hoop. A smaller crossbar near the bottom of the post drags two boulders on short chains over the flat rock. Chunks of ore and a few pans of water are then thrown in.

A raster. The same, ancient principle of rock against rock, to break, to grind, to pulverize. But this time without Indians or mules. Water, wood, and stone do the job, and the ore mined in a day can be milled during the night. In this fashion, one miner with a few tools and a burro can run his own operation. These brown men gathered around me in the shade grin and gesture graphically as they describe their work. They appear happy with their lot, despite the miserable sums they earn, because what they have is entirely their own. That is what life is about, they say. *¡El mejor es, vivir a su gusto en su tierra!*

One of the miners produces a small bottle and coaxes from it a tiny, heavy ball, white as chalk-dust. He places it in my palm and they all smile at me expectantly, as if this pellet were a living baby. Gold. Panned from the concentrate in the raster, it is mingled with mercury, which separates it from traces of grit, and the resultant mix is then heated to recover the gold. The retorting is imperfect and leaves a white film of quicksilver; but this is essentially solid gold, a soft, heavy nib weighing perhaps an ounce. Two months or more of hard work.

In all the deliberations over the Blue Ridge project, the Homestake company never provided for the good commissioners a single grain of their product, except for what glinted from the cuffs and ties of their representatives. And in my life as a United States citizen I have never seen a single gram of that eight or ten thousand tons of the stuff that keeps my dollars strong. Here is an interesting difference between twentieth-century America and the ancient world. In the time of Hatshepsut, around 1500 B.C., the royal wealth of Egypt was openly, flamboyantly displayed. Gold was considered sacred, the very body of Amon-Re the sun god, and the Pharaohs of the eighteenth dynasty sat on golden thrones, ate from golden platters, and traveled on gold-sheathed barges.

Even in such company, Hatshepsut was a queen inordinately fond of appearance. She surrounded herself with the divine metal, beaten into thin sheets, woven into fabrics, drawn into filigree. She powdered her face with gold dust for state occasions and, at the height of her power, planned to erect two mighty obelisks of pure gold over her temple at Karnak. The frantic royal treasurer finally dissuaded her—there was not enough gold in the known world to erect such monuments—and she settled for two stone columns covered in gold plate. The same ostentation characterized Croesus in ancient Delphi, the Roman emperors, and Montezuma and Atahualpa in the New World. These royal persons appeared always in a glittering context of gold, and even the Spaniards who had seen Charles V's court were stunned by the opulence of the Aztec and Inca rulers.

The dazzle of all these monarchs taken together is nevertheless piddling compared to the resources of the United States government. That famous room, filled as high as the Atahualpa could reach with gold trinkets, contained a mere twenty-four tons, while our national reserves in 1980 amounted to more than eight thousand tons—down, as I said, from the twenty-two thousand tons stockpiled before 1950. But we average citizens will never see any of this vast hoard. Our enlightened civilization skips the whole business of public display, and as soon as the gold is refined it is again entombed in the earth from which it came. In the form of small, plain bars it squats in deep vaults of reinforced concrete and steel, sealed with complicated electronic time locks and guarded by heavily armed men. If it moves, it usually travels by forklift, conveyor belt, and armored vehicle, supervised by teams of clerks who wear steel booties to protect their feet in case an ingot is dropped. (None of the agony and despair of a sore toe here!) Almost all of it will remain in these underground chambers, forever hidden from the sight of common persons. No dishes or furniture or even jewelry is fabricated from this treasure, and no president casts a crown or scepter from it.

All the same, gold exerts its power from these subterranean vaults, and it is ultimately the same power the Egyptians and Aztecs and Incas knew, that dark glow of death. I don't mean the obsession with decorating crypts, carrying rings and fans and flagons into the next world. I refer to the authority of the state, that license by which one man—king, chancellor, magistrate— can dispose of the lives of others. In a word, slavery. This ultimate mastery, once a bright circle on the brow of a king, is now compacted into plain metal bars hidden in underground fortresses.

In Hatshepsut's time the connection was explicit, straightforward. To get the rare gold—Egypt soon exhausted her own supply—expeditions were launched into the harsh, barren Kush. The expeditions consisted of captains, camel drivers, guards, and slaves. The caravans took scant rations, and sometimes only half the slaves made it to the mines, where the survivors were systematically worked to death. Only the captains, guards, and the gold-laden pack trains returned. This system endured nearly two thousand years; a half-century before Christ the Greek historian Diodorus visited the mines of the Kush and vividly described how men, women, and children were still driven by the lash until they dropped, while many others died of thirst so that precious water could be conserved to wash the gold.

Rome was no better. In the Pyrenees are abandoned mines lined with iron rings where Iberian and Nubian slaves were chained, and great heaps of human bones can be found in the shafts. Like the Egyptians, Greeks, Persians, and Scythians that preceded them, and the Byzantine and New World kings who came after, the Romans loved egomaniacal ostentation and would invade, murder, and enslave to get the gold which was the most obvious, visible embodiment of pomp. Many of their conquests—Egypt, Gaul, Iberia—were no more than raids to obtain gold and slaves.

The crowns, breastplates, bracelets, and temple domes of precious metal in turn acted as guarantees of authority. By means of rich gifts the Caesars purchased warriors and supplies for their raids, or the craftsmen and materials for sumptuous accoutrements; and logically enough, an exquisite necklace hung on the emperor's wife helped convince the dubious that the master could be counted on to launch profitable new ventures. Returning from their forays in distant lands, the Roman generals paraded their loot in the streets—the chained slaves and the wagonloads of gold treasures—as a signal to the senators of renewed power and influence.

In political life, the Romans forged a notorious bond between gold and blood. The Senate offered to buy the head of Caius Gracchus with gold of an equal weight, and Sulla Felix offered ten thousand dollars a head (literally) for his enemies within the realm, whom he proscribed by the thousands. The Praetorian Guard accepted countless bribes, betraying and executing one emperor after another. Hostile barbarians understood this dynamic well enough. When Crassus, the richest Roman of the first triumvirate and Julius Caesar's principal creditor, launched an inept expedition of his own to Carrhae, the Parthians captured him and, aware of his obsession, poured molten gold down his throat.

Our American prospector, our sourdough, the independent crank with only a grubstake and a dream to drive him, is a rare aberration in the history of mining. For most of human history bright gold has been wrested from the bowels of the earth by the captive and condemned. Even in the last century slaves and convicts dug much of the world's gold. The placer deposits in Siberia were worked first by serfs, then by Stalin's political prisoners, who brought in enough to make Russia the world's second largest producer.

Most of this terrible labor, however, has been performed by dark-skinned people. The Spaniard's reliance on Indian slaves has already been remarked. To keep the Andean mines operating they shipped men in chains from the Caribbean and Central American jungles, so depopulating much of that region that they were forced to import new slaves from Africa to work the plantations. Even today, of the 472,000 gold miners at work in the world, 428,000 are black migrant laborers in South Africa who live and toil under conditions most employees in modern industrial states would find intolerable. Mining is like other dangerous and dirty jobs; it is most often done by the wretched of the earth.

So the true reagents in the crucible are not mercury and cyanide but sweat and blood. The bones of suffering men, millions upon millions of them, have gone to feed the smelters, and the pick-and-shovel symbol that marks a mine for the cartographer could with justice be replaced by the manacle and lash. The other side of this ghastly equation is of course the history of indulgence, license, excess, and perversion that characterizes the great gold-gobbling civilizations. One suspects that for the likes of Caligula, Nero, and Elagabalus, the misery of their slaves is the final titillation, the final depravity; that the wealthy patrician's wife who dons a ring or diadem of pure gold senses, with a deep, obscure thrill, the presence of those dark underground legions who have been sacrificed in its making.

After Anicleto Junior has dumped his sack of ore into the tauna along with a few panfuls of water, we return to the trail and follow it to the family estate. The house, an unprepossessing adobe structure with a hard-packed dirt floor, is located at a rare point where the canyon widens into a low bench above the river. Here Anicleto has planted his garden, and a small marvel it is. There are indeed oranges and lemons, and also limes, pomegranates, grapes, avocados, peaches, apricots, figs, and apples—all watered by a cold, crystal spring that cascades out of the cliffside. Only a few yards away Anicleto shows me a second spring, equally clear but just warm to the hand. Very nice in the winter, he observes, and you should see the clouds of steam!

The pathways between orchard plots are planted with roses, marigolds, pansies, and snapdragons, and there is a good-sized field of corn, squash, beans, tomatoes, and peppers. A scatter of chickens wanders there, pecking after insects. We get enough here, Anicleto says, to feed all nine of us. All these trees, I say in wonder, how did they get here? I carried them in, he replies. On your back? He smiles. Of course.

I notice a neat stack of freshly cut firewood by the door as we enter the house, and see that it goes to feed the stove against one wall, where Anicleto's daughter, a beautiful thirteen-year-old, is patting tortillas to lay out on the iron plate supported by mud brick walls. She gives me a shy, terrified smile and the smacking of dough against palm picks up in pace. I am introduced first to the mother, a thickset woman, very Indian of countenance and already white-haired. She nods and greets me formally, but does not stop cranking on the hand mill which is grinding the corn into fresh flour for the tortillas. Next the younger sons, nine and twelve, who regard me with dour, unsmiling intensity, and then another daughter, sixteen, emerges from an adjoining room after a sharp prompting from her father. She is gawky and uncomfortable in the green sack dress which I suspect she has just donned, and cannot look at me.

The eldest son has been spooning soup and wolfing down tortillas at the table, but now looks up to acknowledge me. His father mentions that he is twenty-five. Since Anicleto has already told me he is only forty-one, I am impressed with the size and range of his brood, all raised here in the Barranca, where there is no sign of the facilities we North Americans hold to be so

165

essential: electricity, telephones, doctors, pharmacies, fire brigades, police departments, and, of course, banks. On the other hand, there is in this humble household an exemplary form of communal purpose and mutual assistance. Anicleto Junior arrives, having put the burro in the corral, and even as his step is heard on the stones outside the elder daughter serves up a bowl of soup and the younger delivers beside it a stack of tortillas hot off the stove.

At a word from the father I am supplied with lemonade, then coffee, and finally *tesguino*, a homemade beer brewed from corn, very much like the *chicha* of the Andean people. This drink must indeed be very old in the Americas; it is rich, nourishing, packs a definite wallop, and can be brewed fresh in a matter of days. It goes well enough with the tortillas, much thicker than the machine-made ones but easier to chew, for the flour is coarse and crumbly. Around mouthfuls I talk with the Anicletos—the father and middle son are clearly the voluble ones—about gold, work, hardship, money, and children.

The estimates on economic matters are vague, heavily qualified. They sometimes do better than two grams a week, or nearly twenty dollars, but also there are weeks of less than a gram. They know the current international price of gold, and receive from their buyers about half that sum. The problem is, of course, the unstable peso, worth less and less by the day. But that is good for me, is it not, since my dollars buy more and more? The technological advancement of the United States is no doubt responsible. Also the corruption in the Mexican government. Still, we agree, there is some profound mystery in all this: gold, currency, prices, politics. Presumably someone somewhere understands the subtle connections among these things. What is certain here is simply that the best thing is to live as one pleases in his own land. *¡A su gusto en su tierra!* Here they have enough to eat from the garden and chicken house, so they need cash only for shoes, axes, cigarettes—things of this sort. So saying, Anicleto offers me another Faro.

It is mid-afternoon by now. I recall that I have a hard three-hour haul in front of me, and am inspired to ask if, perhaps, Anicleto Junior could be persuaded to transport me to the canyon rim on a burro for—I aim at what seems generous but not lavish—eight hundred pesos. The young man breaks into his wide grin and utters a yelp of delight. Of course! Why not? He receives a sagacious nod from his father, and tells me, on his way to the door, that they have a very good animal for the job, if he can be located. It will be simple, easy, no problem.

I finish my beer, pay Anicleto Senior the eight hundred, and express my appreciation for this hospitality. Everyone in the room, except the two youngest boys, smiles at me. I judge by an indefinable slight change in Mama's manner that the sum I have named is right. Anicleto tells me he has enjoyed our talk, and invites me to return some day for a longer visit. They do not get much company, he adds with a wry look. He comes to the door with me, where Anicleto Junior has brought the burro, the same one who bore the ore sacks on the trail. The other one—the better of the two—has run off up the trail, Junior says. We will watch for him and switch mounts when we can. You must hurry, his father says with a glance at the shadow on the canyon wall, or you will have to spend the night up there.

The boy shrugs and gestures to me, so I approach the burro. The animal is knob-kneed, barrel-bodied and even smaller than Gutierrez's horse, impossibly small for my bulk. Only its ears are of impressive size, and it is lovely only for the soft, chocolate nap on its hide and for large, dark eyes. A blanket has been folded and placed across the wooden packsaddle, but there are no stirrups. A good thing, for once athwart the beast I find that I can touch my toes to the ground on either side. Anicleto Junior does not seem perturbed at this disproportion; he hands me the rope halter, takes up a position behind me and with a slap on the burro's rump heads us along the trail.

The small hooves click on the rock and the great ears bob before me, until we reach the base of the first pitch up the river bank and there the burro drifts to a stop. A drumming of heels against his ribs, a gee-up or two and we make the first switchback. Then he stops again. This time more kicking and ki-ying are required. Anicleto takes a few moments to show me how to haul on the rope halter and cuts a short switch so I can smack little clouds of dust from the rump and flanks. But within a hundred yards we are at a full halt again.

Anicleto cuts a second switch for himself, and between the two of us we get the beast moving, but now he will march only under a continual rain of blows and curses. I am not delivering my commands, my guide hints, with sufficient authority. Before long this flailing seems to me more exhausting than carrying my own weight. I try to explain this to Anicleto, but he is dismayed by the idea. Jerk his head, hit him with the switch, and say the following swear words, he instructs.

It is no use. In sheer frustration and weariness, I dismount. *"No funciona,"* I announce. Not worth the trouble. Why not unsaddle him and drive him back down the trail homeward. Anicleto looks woeful.

"Por favor, Señor—¡monte!" he says. Keep at it. Bear down on the switch.

"No funciona," I insist firmly. I try not to appear reproachful, but adopt rather the manner of the grand, forgiving seigneur. In point of fact, eight hundred pesos is nothing to me, a willing contribution to a poor, deserving family. The noblesse of the strong dollar obliges.

Anicleto apologizes profusely and tries to encourage me with the resourceful suggestion that we will be able to track the other burro—a much superior animal, he insists, for he has not been cut—and after switching the saddle we can ride on without further difficulties.

I conceal my deep doubt of any such outcome, but march onward hauling the burro by his halter. Though the climb will be even slower this way, I am glad for company. Twice more Anicleto pleads with me, persuades me to climb on the animal briefly, but the result is always the same: a few dozen yards at a lethargic gait, ever more frequent pauses, ending finally in obdurate immobility.

Not quite half way to the top, climbing now in the shadow of night—even though the canyon rim is still a splendid rose-gold—Anicleto spies the other burro in a clump of mesquite on a narrow terrace off the trail. He unlashes a coil of rope from the packsaddle and darts into the brush, motioning me to block the trail on the downhill side. Before long I hear a rattle of hooves and thrashing of branches, then an exclamation of triumph. Anicleto emerges on the trail again, beaming proudly with his prize in tow.

If the first steed was homely, this second one is actually grotesque. The rotund body is wholly out of proportion to the stumpy legs, and it has lost half of one ear in some youthful combat. Its dusty black hair is stiff as wire and matted with burrs. The expression about the eyes is at once savage and sinister.

"*Eso es macho,*" Anicleto says with happy grin. "*Fuerte.*" I do not appear impressed, but he grins more widely yet. "*Funciona,*" he says gaily. "*Monte.*"

I sigh, hitch up my trousers and mount bareback, headed up the trail. Anicleto releases the rope from about its neck and with the knotted end flogs the burro once on the hindquarters, uttering at the same time a sharp whistle.

I nearly topple over backwards as the animal breaks into an instantaneous gallop, then plunge forward to dig my fingers into the muscular neck. Four hooves are clattering like a chain running through a block, and branches slash at my head and shoulders. The burro hits a switchback without a pause. I can feel the thick little body bunch like a fist under me.

I am shouting mindless admonitions to stop, slow up, let me off, but I hear Anicleto's huaraches smacking in a fast run behind me, urging the burro on. "*¿Funciona? ¿Funciona?*" I hear him hollering in wild glee. "*¡Eso es macho!*"

Through the last tunnel of branches the macho torpedo spies something that puzzles him, so he stops like a truck colliding with a tree. I just manage to convert my own momentum into an ambiguous, windmilling descent. Anicleto trots up with a whoop of laughter, still hauling the other burro behind.

"*¡Eh, señor! ¡Macho!* What did I tell you? He functions, no?"

I have to laugh along with him. I cannot be offended, whatever the risk to my old bones, at such an eruption of energy. The saddle is quickly transferred and the brown burro driven back down the trail toward home. Gingerly I hoist a leg over the new mount and we are off at a near trot. Anicleto hurrying to keep up.

This dark thunderbolt is Mocha de Juarez, Anicleto informs me proudly. Old one-ear. Actually he is only two years old, but he has already proved his strength, boldness and endurance. I find it little short of miraculous that, without faltering, he can boost my eighty and more kilos nearly straight up over broken, sharp rock. If anything, my weight seems to provide a convenient ballast against which he can set his masculine shoulders and drive the mountain away under him with piston-strokes of his hooves. The muscles I touch on his neck feel like steel cable.

Macho. The word has fallen into disrepute among my countrypersons, carrying connotations of oppression, ignorant arrogance, and false pretense. In this new context I find in it an original significance of raw, straightforward power. Here is the best reflection of the indomitable conquistador and the fierce Indian, a compaction of force that served either indiscriminately and may very well outlast both.

We are climbing now briskly and steadily through cooler air, for clouds have materialized suddenly. At first they are scattered, cottony puffs but soon pile into gray-shadowed tiers and towers. A crack of thunder, and I feel the dense stillness that precedes a downpour. The sun has set spectacularly, leaving a broad band of salmon red behind the dark cliffs. Across the great gulf of canyon, veils of rain drift down from the clouds, and in their blue caverns appear now and then spidery cracks of lightning.

Near the rim, Anicleto turns us into a shortcut, a faint trail almost straight up. Even Mocha must scramble here, and at such an angle I can no longer maintain my seat, even after throwing both arms around his neck. We reach a narrow ledge and stop for a breath. I see a cave entrance across which a low wooden door has been rigged. On the ground beside the door are a couple of cheap pots. A Tarahumara home, either abandoned or awaiting

170

summer occupancy. When I glance over at Anicleto, I see him walk to the cave entrance, open his fly, and—incredibly—begin pissing on the threshold.

I stare as he finishes, shakes himself, buttons up quickly, and comes back to the trail. He says nothing, shows no sign of either guilt or satisfaction, does not remark my deliberate stare. Clucking at Mocha, he resumes the climb, and after a moment I expel a held breath and follow. In twenty minutes, sometimes proceeding hand over hand up the rocky ravine or—in Mocha's case—springing from crag to ledge like a goat, we reach the summit. Anicleto removes the saddle, blanket, and rope from Mocha, and with a shout and a wave, the boy sends our macho express back down the trail at a gallop.

We emerge at a point only a few hundred yards from our original campsite. Manuel has stacked all our gear carefully under the tree, saddles and grub under the blankets. There is no sign of him or the horses, and for a moment I am uneasy. But when the first few drops, large and wet, splatter on the dry stone around us, Manuel arrives, leading our mounts through the gloom. He has, he announces, been in search of pasturage again.

Introductions over, we set about locating a new quick camp in the darkness. Our former site on the rim is obviously too dangerous in a lightning storm. Manuel and Anicleto agree that one of the old building shells, without roof, would be some protection from the wind. We find a suitable one and clear the rubble from the earthen floor. Anicleto insists on stacking the usable stones in an empty doorway as a windbreak, pointing out that the next travelers will appreciate this gesture.

A fire is quickly struck in the middle of our room and I dig out the last of our supplies: a can of tuna, another of ham, a cup of rice, an onion, and a few spoons of salsa. Fortunately one of the twelve-ounce bottles of yellow, iodized water remains. The raindrops, though huge, remain scattered, and soon the wind is ripping the fire into bright pennants that push the darkness out of our chamber. I pour the water in a small pot and hang it on a stick over the blaze.

Manuel and Anicleto, after a period of guarded exchanges, grow voluble and competitive. Saying nothing of his Tarahumara blood, Manuel is playing the urban sophisticate, mentioning that he has seen not only Chihuahua but Mexico City. With a kind of perverse pride, he mentions that he never knew his father and has managed on his own. Anicleto responds genially that he has spent his whole life at the bottom of the canyon with his family, except for rare trips to Creel and once to Chihuahua. He declares that they are quite content with the independence conferred by the little vein of gold, their garden and chickens and burros.

Manuel shrugs and observes that, still, there is no television and that is something serious. Television is wonderful. But here is wonderful, too, Anicleto rejoins and I second him. Even this dirt-floored ruin has become cheerful, and the pot, into which I have emptied everything, is simmering with a savory promise. We can't stay, Manuel reminds me, because there is no pasture and no more food after this. No roof, either, since the Indians tore everything down.

There is again disagreement over the origin of these structures. Manuel claims adamantly that the inhabitants were troops sent in to combat the bandidos, the marijuana runners. Anicleto remains dubious, arguing that the large mining corporations must have been responsible. Not that anyone doubts the existence of armed marauders. The boys agree vehemently on the perennial presence of this species here in Chihuahua, which was, after all, Pancho Villa's stronghold. Great wars have been fought here, and recently, they tell me. Twenty truckloads of soldiers, machine guns and howitzers, an aerial combat involving—Manuel hesitates in concentration—thirty fighter planes. The marijuana kings commanded as many as five hundred warriors, but all these were killed, captured, or dispersed.

Anicleto has forgotten the mining companies. A certain man who lives nearby escaped from the *federales*, he says, even though a hundred of them surprised him at a distance of no more than three paces, as close as from me to you. This certain man, one revolver stuck in his belt fore, another aft, a knife in his boot and his carbine in his hands, dodged and ran like a deer, firing rounds over his shoulder, and escaped into the Barranca.

I cannot help observing that the expense for such massive manoeuvers seems inordinate, given the state of Mexico's economy. Also it is hard to believe this common narcotic weed seriously threatens the stability of the social order.

The boys remonstrate that these are robbers by trade and dangerous hombres by disposition. They steal everything, Manuel asserts. And high on this smoke, Anicleto adds eagerly, they kill indiscriminately. The señor should remember that tremendous amounts of money are involved—even in dollars. A big business. Why, Manuel says, marijuana is so plentiful here they feed it sometimes to their horses, and thus rendered loco, these horses will kill a dog—or even a man—if they encounter one on the trail. Anicleto, eyes flashing in the firelight, demonstrates how they rear and strike with their hooves.

The wind is coming now in big, cool gusts that set the pines roaring, but there is no more rain. I can see a patch or two of stars above. In and around our conversation we have dispatched the spicy mixture of rice, meat, and onion. Now Anicleto feeds a few branches of pine to the coals and opens another pack of the cheap cigarettes. He and Manuel are propped against the saddles, blankets over their shoulders, ready for matching stories far into the night.

I have enough wild tales to occupy my dreams. From my grandfather's last disgusted look over his shoulder at the old miner, standing in his cabin doorway with foot and throat newly bandaged, through the intricate turns of politics behind the gold hoards of our Free World Democracies, to this camp-fire in a desert wilderness where young men dream of danger, is as far as I want to go into the mystery of human aspiration on this continent. I am satisfied that in some dislocated and oblique way the deadly patterns are still with us, still virulent. Men obsessed with the power of death, the heavy radiance of gold, are still laboring in a frenzy to acquire, to wield, to triumph. In hopelessness a few may still cut their own throats. It is possible no moun-tain, no forest, no river can survive their onslaught; no alien and backward race thwart their desire. I cannot even find a ready way to blame them. I know only that I rejoice in this earth's most desolate, final places where a few hungry aboriginals live differently and perhaps scheme to make an occasional raid, pull down a few stones, or sell a forbidden weed.

The general opinion is that these descendants of the first Americans will not endure long. Their extermination and assimilation proceed apace in Mexico, El Salvador, Guatemala, Nicaragua, Brazil, Colombia, Peru. Still, if the balance of payments should ever shift significantly, if we have not quite enough helicopters and laser-guided missiles and frag bombs to protect our vaults of gold and vigorous dollars, if the ragged hordes who stare through plate glass at withered gringos dining so resplendently should sense an uncertainty, a vulnerability . . . *¿Quien sabe?* It is true they have only burros and machetes, a few ancient shotguns. But I can vouchsafe to my fellow North Americans that in their own land, living as they wish, they are macho; very definitely, they function.

I unroll my down bag and bid my companions good night, glad to settle a weary and aching body against this hard earth and drift toward sleep. I will be attended by the steady purling of Spanish, the flutter of the fire, and an occasional roll of distant thunder.

PHOTOGRAPHS

Page 13: The results of two fishing expeditions in Idaho, probably early twentieth century. (Idaho Historical Society.)

Pages 14–15: Fishing with a serviceberry branch on Big Bear Creek, 1908. (Idaho Historical Society.)

Pages 22–23: Logging crew at unidentified location, probably northern Idaho. (Idaho Historical Society.)

Pages 26–27: Erma Schultz Harland's beauty shop, Troy, Idaho, 1935. (Idaho Historical Society.)

Page 38: The author's father (at right) and companions with a dead bear. (Family photograph.)

Pages 46–47: The author's father (center) with fellow workers at sawmill. (Family photograph.)

Page 53: Aunt Nellie and Uncle Jess. (Family photograph.)

Pages 66–67: Mining camp in the mountains of Idaho. (Idaho Historical Society.)

Pages 84–85: *Landscape near Unadilla,* Lynn Dance, 1976. (Sheldon Memorial Art Gallery, University of Nebraska–Lincoln; gift of the artist.)

Page 88: Big Foot in death, photographed at the Wounded Knee battlefield. (Smithsonian Institution, photograph no. 55,018.)

Pages 92, 104: Ashaninka Indians. (Author's photographs.)

Pages 122–23: The Caswell brothers, discoverers of Thunder Mountain, in their cabin. (Idaho Historical Society.)

Page 152: Sourdough panning gold. (Idaho Historical Society.)